A Killing in
Real Estate

A Killing in Real Estate

ROBERT UPTON

An Amos McGuffin Mystery

A DUTTON BOOK

DUTTON

Published by the Penguin Group
Penguin Books USA Inc., 375 Hudson Street,
New York, New York 10014, U.S.A.
Penguin Books Ltd, 27 Wrights Lane, London W8 5TZ, England
Penguin Books Australia Ltd, Ringwood, Victoria, Australia
Penguin Books Canada Ltd, 2801 John Street,
Markham, Ontario, Canada L3R 1B4
Penguin Books (N.Z.) Ltd, 182-190 Wairau Road, Auckland 10, New Zealand

Penguin Books Ltd, Registered Offices:
Harmondsworth, Middlesex, England

First published by Dutton, an imprint of New American Library,
a division of Penguin Books USA Inc.
Distributed in Canada by McClelland & Stewart Inc.

First Printing, December, 1990
10 9 8 7 6 5 4 3 2 1

REGISTERED TRADEMARK—MARCA REGISTRADA

LIBRARY OF CONGRESS CATALOGING IN PUBLICATION DATA:

Upton, Robert.
   A killing in real estate : an Amos McGuffin mystery / Robert
Upton.
      p.   cm.
   ISBN 0-525-24927-3
   I. Title.
PS3571.P5K55   1990
813'.54—dc20   90-45765
                                                         CIP

Printed in the United States of America
Set in Times Roman

PUBLISHER'S NOTE
This is a work of fiction. Names, characters, places, and incidents either are
the product of the author's imagination or are used fictitiously, and any
resemblance to actual persons, living or dead, events, or locales is entirely
coincidental.

To Pat, again

A Killing in
Real Estate

Chapter 1

He looked at her and smiled when her hand squeezed his. The rapt expression on her beautiful upturned face as she stared intently at the performers onstage was one he had never seen before. And as he watched her he began to worry that exposing her to this at so early and innocent an age might have been a dreadful mistake. Until now he had been able to exert some influence and control over her, but he could see as he watched her eyes widen at the performance of the governess with her young charges that her innocence was giving way to a disturbing awareness of possibilities beyond his own ambitions for her. Sensing that something must be done, he leaned close and whispered in her ear, "It's only pretend."

"Daddy!" she said, rolling her eyes with such dismay as only a young daughter can summon when confronted by the hopelessly uncool opinion of so embarrassingly square a father as Amos McGuffin. Her mother was an actress, for God's sake, with the Actors Company of New York, doing the governess in *The Cherry Orchard*, for God's sake.

McGuffin released his daughter's hand and slumped in his seat. He was right, bringing Hillary here was a grave tactical error. As was hanging around New York week after week, listening to his ex-wife's excuses for not allowing him to take his daughter back to San Francisco (where by law she belonged) "just yet." He should have gone straight to a lawyer and had Marilyn arrested for kidnapping.

1

Every day Hillary was becoming more and more a New Yorker, and he was partly, if unwittingly, to blame. While Marilyn had rehearsed *The Cherry Orchard*, McGuffin showed Hillary the sights—Coney Island, the aquarium, Central Park, the Bronx Zoo, Aqueduct, Yankee Stadium, Broadway, Greenwich Village, Soho, The Plaza, Radio City, FAO Schwarz—all the good stuff. That was dumb. Why didn't I show her the subway, the South Bronx, a welfare hotel, Rikers Island—the real New York? And now this, a New York play featuring her mother, even if only in a minor role.

It was all a New York hustle, McGuffin was sure. Marilyn was invited from San Francisco to join the once-prestigious Actors Company, now an expensive diploma mill, simply because she was willing to pay dearly for the privilege of studying acting with the school's director, Franz Tutin. Although several stars had passed through the Actors Company on their way to Hollywood fame, and their names appeared prominently in all the school's promotional materials, there were thousands of others for whom it had only been a waste of time and money. And Marilyn, McGuffin feared, was destined to be one of these. But try telling that to a little girl who was suddenly no less star-struck than her mother.

As the sound of chopping and falling cherry trees grew in the distance, McGuffin stole a sad sideways glance at his daughter. There was no mistaking that look. He had seen it in her mother before, first as a struggling painter, then a poet, then a singer, and now finally a New York actress. Not for Hillary the gritty real world of nine to five, mortgages, two-week paid vacations and Christmases with Dad. Hillary had been tonight tapped by Thespis and McGuffin had lost a daughter to the stage.

He was roused from the sad contemplation of his loss by the applause signaling the end of the opening-night performance. Although unfamiliar with New York theater audiences, to him their response to the play seemed somewhat tepid. This was confirmed as he led Hillary up the aisle and

2

threaded his way through the crowded foyer, listening to the snippets of negative opinion that floated on the air like something foul smelling.

"If I see *The Cherry Orchard* one more time—"

"Wherever did they get that governess?"

"California."

"I'm not surprised."

If the governess's daughter heard any unkind comments—and McGuffin doubted that in her present state of rapture she could hear anything over the chorus of muses buzzing in her brain—she gave no indication.

"How did you like it?" he asked, once in the cab and on their way to the cast party.

"It was the most wonderful thing in my whole life," she answered.

"That good, huh," McGuffin said, peering out the window. For so prestigious a group as the Actors Company, its headquarters, a crumbling stone church surrounded by dilapidated tenements in the west Forties, seemed an unlikely temple to the actor's art.

"Do you know what I want to be when I grow up?" she asked, slipping her hand in his.

"A San Francisco fireperson?"

"Oh, Daddy!" Tugging at his hand. "I want to be an actress."

"Fine, you can be a San Francisco actress."

"Not a San Francisco actress, Daddy," she said, thoroughly disgusted. "I want to be a New York actress—like Mommy."

"But wouldn't you like to be in the movies?"

"Oh, I will be," she assured him.

"Well, San Francisco is right next to Hollywood. If you lived there you'd always be available when the good roles were being cast."

"I suppose that's true," she said thoughtfully. Then, having arrived at her first important career decision, she announced, "But I prefer to learn my craft on the stage."

McGuffin groaned inwardly as the cab drew to a stop in front of Sardi's.

3

"The party's in the Belasco Room," Hillary said when he started for the wrong door.

"You seem very familiar here," McGuffin observed, as the elevator doors closed.

"Mommy and I have lunch here all the time," she explained.

"Is that right," McGuffin mumbled, calculating the cost as the door slid open. The bar at one end of the Belasco Room was already crowded with first nighters. "Wait right here," he instructed.

"Remember, Mommy said not to drink too much," she cautioned.

"Yeah, yeah—" McGuffin muttered, as he threaded his way to the bar. The woman is guilty of felony kidnapping and she has the audacity to lecture me about the evils of alcohol.

By waving a ten-dollar bill at the barman he was able to move up several places in line and return quickly with a Coke and a full tumbler of scotch. Both McGuffins sipped their drinks and picked through the crowd for stars, finding none. He finished his quickly then returned to the bar where the barman with a good memory quickly refilled his glass with scotch.

A spark from near the door ignited a blaze of applause that rolled across the room as Franz Tutin strode in imperiously, followed by his aspiring student actors, in descending order of importance. Marilyn was the last to enter.

"Doesn't Mommy look beautiful?" Hillary asked.

"Gorgeous," McGuffin answered. And she did.

"I'm going to congratulate her," she said, dashing off.

Marilyn saw him and waved. McGuffin gave her a thumbs-up and she smiled uncertainly. Being the new girl on the block and not wanting to upstage the stars, she had dressed simply in a long black velvet skirt and a white silk blouse, allowing her long blond hair to trail where it may, but her chosen bushel basket did nothing to conceal her light. Watching her work the room, effortlessly charming all within her pale, McGuffin wondered why he was no longer

4

living with such a woman. Until a short while later, when she approached with her star-struck daughter at her side.

"Doing your best to get drunk, I see," she said privately without breaking her smile.

"Ask Hilly, this is my second drink," McGuffin defended, as Marilyn locked her arm in his and steered him to the vestibule behind the bar.

"Don't you mean second pint?" she corrected, pushing him through the doorway.

"I'm merely celebrating your splendid performance," he replied.

"Thank you, darling. But if you truly do wish me well, don't spoil it for me by getting drunk, okay?"

"Have you seen me drunk since I've been in New York?"

"No, but we both know the reason for that, don't we?"

"If you think I'm on my best behavior only so I can take Hillary back to San Francisco, you're woefully mistaken," he informed her. "Because I could get as drunk as a skunk, but it wouldn't change the terms of our custody agreement."

"Amos, could we discuss this at another time?" Marilyn pleaded, while beaming a brave smile back into the room. They were partly concealed, but it wasn't nearly enough.

"When? I've been hanging around for weeks listening to one excuse after another. You promised Hillary could go back after you opened and—"

"That's not what I said!"

"It is what you said and I intend to leave with Hillary tomorrow!"

"You'll do no such thing!" she said, pulling Hillary to her.

"Tomorrow morning I'm either going to the airport or to a lawyer—it's up to you!"

"Daddy—" Hillary groaned, mortified at the attention she imagined they were drawing.

"Your mother and I are discussing your future," McGuffin informed her in a reasonable voice before turning back to her mother. "So what's it going to be?"

"Amos, please, we'll talk about it later—at my apartment."

"It's always later!" McGuffin began.

"This will be final, I promise. Please, Amos?" she asked. She released Hillary and entwined both arms around his. "This is my big night, don't wreck it, huh?"

McGuffin nodded. "Okay. But no more excuses."

"No more," she pledged, then quickly kissed him on the cheek. "Thank you, darling. And take Hillary home soon, okay?"

"But, Mommy, I want to go with you," Hillary wailed.

She glanced guiltily from the crowd to her daughter. "I know, darling, and I'd love to have you, but it would only confuse people," she said, before kissing her and plunging back into the crowd.

He finished his drink in several quick gulps, then waited while the whiskey worked its own magic. "What'll we do now?" he asked.

"Let's not go home yet," Hillary pleaded.

McGuffin regarded the empty glass in his hand. Maybe one more, he decided. "You want another drink?"

"I still have one," she said, holding her glass up for inspection.

"Then go out and mingle," McGuffin said. "And if anybody asks who you are, you tell them you're Marilyn McGuffin's younger sister."

"Oh, Daddy!" she said, grinning but loving the idea.

Then she struck out into the crowd with all the aplomb of her mother, gathering the attention of jaded New York theatergoers as easily as picking flowers in a garden. It had begun to occur to McGuffin, not without considerable pain, that Marilyn might be right, that Hillary might thrive in New York, might attain something unavailable, or at least far less accessible, in San Francisco. It was at first an alien notion, hopelessly encumbered by a preconceived idea of Manhattan as a filthy, crime-ridden, concrete jail with lousy weather—all of which was true—but there were also things so compelling about the city that even an old San Francisco hand like McGuffin was in danger of being seduced. It was a city where things got done, bad and good. There was an

6

activity for everybody, actor, painter, writer, con man, swindler, hustler, salesman, broker, politician, extortionist, contortionist, exhibitionist, lunatic, saint, killer or healer. Just the buzz of activity that will never engage him, or the opportunities he'll never take, are as comforting to the New Yorker as the great outdoors is to the naturalist. And McGuffin was beginning to feel the buzz. He knew he shouldn't have another drink, but Hillary was having too much fun for him to pull her away now, he rationalized. And besides, there was a tuxedoed waiter standing beside him with nothing to do.

"Fill it up with your best scotch," McGuffin instructed, thrusting the empty glass and a ten-dollar bill on the man. "And don't worry, I'm not performing tonight," he added, when the waiter hesitated.

When the waiter returned a few minutes later, McGuffin took the drink and tried to stuff another ten in his hand.

"I've already been most generously rewarded," the waiter said, refusing the ten.

"Make hay while the sun shines," McGuffin advised, as he stuffed the bill into the waiter's breast pocket.

McGuffin heard his name and turned. It was Marilyn, ashen-faced, making for him. "What are you doing?" she demanded.

"Just having a drink," he answered.

"I'm so sorry, Mr. Belmont—I hope he hasn't—"

"Not at all," Mr. Belmont said, removing the bill from his dinner jacket.

"Belmont—?" McGuffin repeated, as he spotted Franz Tutin moving toward him.

"Victor, is everything all right?" Tutin asked, in a deep-voiced middle-European accent.

"Everything is fine," Victor assured them. "In fact if I had known waiters were this well paid I might never have gone into real estate," he added, extending two ten-dollar bills for McGuffin.

McGuffin looked at the bills, then at the man holding them. "You're not a waiter."

"I'm afraid not. But I am grateful," he added.

"The tux fooled me," McGuffin apologized, pocketing the twenty dollars.

Victor Belmont smiled. "I'll mention that to my tailor."

"Mr. Belmont is the chairman of the Actors Company Foundation," Franz Tutin informed McGuffin, while Marilyn groaned faintly.

"Amos McGuffin," the detective said, extending his hand.

"Marilyn's husband," Tutin explained.

"Ex!" she said quickly.

"Another actor?" Belmont asked, shaking McGuffin's hand.

"Private investigator."

Victor Belmont was amused. "A private investigator—guilty of mistaken identity?"

McGuffin shrugged. "I'm on vacation. What do you do for a living, sell real estate?"

Marilyn groaned again as Tutin stepped in. "Mr. Belmont has a great many interests."

"And tending bar is not one of them," McGuffin said. "Sorry about that, Victor."

"Forget it."

"Let me buy you a drink," McGuffin offered, reaching for his elbow.

"No!" Marilyn fairly screamed, as Tutin's hand fell on McGuffin's arm. "We're going home."

As Marilyn and Franz Tutin pushed him toward the elevator, McGuffin called over his shoulder, "Sorry, Victor, we'll have to have that drink some other time!"

Chapter 2

McGuffin did not return with Hillary to San Francisco the next day as he had vowed, nor did he go to a lawyer as he had threatened. Instead, cowed by guilt and a hangover, he listened uncomplainingly to Marilyn's recitation of his many parental shortcomings.

"And just what exactly is wrong with me?" he had haughtily but foolishly demanded to know. For contrary to the lawyer's maxim, it was sometimes better not to ask a question even when you knew the answer.

"What's wrong!" she repeated. "You drink too much, you hang around Goody's seedy saloon with a bunch of Damon Runyon rejects, you're unconscious, insensitive, and irresponsible; you never know where your next dollar is coming from, and as a father you're only a little less worrisome than a crocodile."

"I know where my next dollar's coming from," McGuffin corrected, referring to the reward for the return of the Fabergé egg, booty from his last case. Faced with the option of selling it to a private collector for a small fortune, or returning it to the Kremlin for a considerably smaller sum, McGuffin had, in the spirit of *perestroika*, opted to return it to the Soviet people. It was not a decision Marilyn had applauded.

"And that's another thing—you're a private investigator, hardly a lucrative profession. So what do you do when you finally have a chance to make some money? You give it away!"

"I didn't give it away," he protested. "The reward is enough for a small trust for my daughter and that's all I need. I make enough to get by."

"Get by— You call two hundred a day plus expenses getting by? Look around you, Amos, what do you see?"

McGuffin did as directed. They were seated in the tiny front room of her third-floor sublet in a Greenwich Village brownstone, bare wood floors, oak furnishings and Laura Ashley curtains on the two front windows, salad days furnishings that depressed him but charmed her. It was a one-year sublet from an actor who was touring Australia in *The Desert Song*, which was a depression of another order.

"No, no—I'm talking about the cosmos," she interrupted, when he began to itemize the contents of her apartment. "I'm talking about ambition, opportunity, the future. Not just Hillary's and mine, but yours as well. New York has more of everything, Amos. More culture, more commerce—"

"More crime."

"Exactly! The crime here, Amos—murder, rape, arson, robbery! And bombs! For instance, the man you sent for a drink last night—do you know who he was?"

"Edward Teller?"

"He's the man whose brother was burned in that explosion the other night. He's probably the richest man in New York, and somebody tried to kill him. If you hadn't been so drunk he might have offered you a job."

McGuffin remembered. Some klutz had been blown up trying to plant a bomb on Victor Belmont's car. Just what I need, a client who's in trouble with the mob. "I'm not interested in getting rich in New York. All I want is a nice quiet life in San Francisco with my daughter. And you if you want to come."

"Is that a reproposal?"

"You know what I mean."

In fact he didn't know himself what he meant. He had been divorced long enough to accept it as his permanent state, yet it sometimes seemed a transitory thing. Although Hillary was the obvious linchpin, McGuffin knew the night

10

he met Marilyn at the No Name Bar in Sausalito that she was not a woman to be easily forgotten. A wasp-waisted, long-legged blonde, she was a painter then, living on a barge on the mud flats, and a far more perfect work herself than any of her canvases. When McGuffin saw her at the bar, surrounded by a gang of hopeful males, he vowed then and there that he would either have her or make fool of himself trying, never realizing that both were possible.

They were married, the detective and the painter, a short while later, and divorced only a few years after that. Marilyn's pursuit of the arts, several of them, left little time for marriage. Tiring of painting, she turned to poetry, then music (singing with a rock group called Stump) and finally the theater. It was there that she truly found herself, after losing McGuffin sometime during her rock period. Yet she too, who blamed McGuffin's career not hers for their breakup, felt that they were bound to somehow always be a part of one another. And that was partly the reason she was trying so hard to keep him in New York.

"What do you think you're doing?" he asked as she stood and began unbuttoning her blouse.

"I know what I'm doing," she said, pulling the blouse from her skirt.

"So do I and it won't work."

McGuffin watched the blouse fall to the floor. Who did she think she was dealing with? While chasing down the Fabergé egg he had been exposed to the blandishments of the beautiful Shawney O'Sea but had never once wavered from the task at hand. Did she seriously believe that the sight of her long-legged, wasp-waisted, full-breasted, naked body would cause him, a tough hard-bitten, inflexibly principled, San Francisco private eye to stray from the course of his duty? Not likely.

"You can knock off the striptease, Marilyn, because I'm not having it. I'm here about Hillary, nothing else. And if you think a quick boff is going to change my mind about taking her home, then I must say, Marilyn, you are sadly guilty of greatly underestimating me."

11

He made a sneering snorting sound meant to convey derision—which also dislodged something in his nose—then snatched a handkerchief from his pocket and quickly blew. When he looked up she was naked, moving toward him, arms outstretched. What the hell, he thought, taking her in his arms. I always knew Spillane was full of shit.

While making love but not yet finished, the phone rang.

"Let it ring—" McGuffin gasped.

"It might be the theater," she said, twisting away and reaching for the phone.

McGuffin waited while she spoke briefly, then with a stunned expression handed him the phone. "It's for you."

"Who is it?" he asked, taking the phone.

"Victor Belmont."

"The waiter?" McGuffin said softly, but not softly enough, as he reached for the phone.

"None other," Victor Belmont said.

"Look, Mr. Belmont, if you're calling for an apology, I'm sorry. Is that enough?"

"Not nearly enough, Mr. McGuffin," he replied. "I'm looking for a private investigator, not an apology."

"I'm a San Francisco PI, not New York," McGuffin informed him.

"Amos!" Marilyn gasped.

"That's precisely why I'm calling," Belmont continued. "The investigation I have in mind requires an anonymous detective."

"Take it!" Marilyn stage-whispered.

"Sorry, I'm going back to San Francisco shortly. With my daughter," he added, looking at Marilyn, who was gesturing imploringly for him to take the job.

"Yes, Franz Tutin mentioned something to me about your problem, Mr. McGuffin. And it occurred to me that we might be able to help each other. I do, after all, retain some of the most expensive lawyers in New York. And I'd also be willing to more than double your fee, just to com-

12

pensate you for being away from home," the millionaire added.

The compensation part flew by almost unnoticed, but the lawyer part caught McGuffin's interest. "Excuse me a moment," he said, then placed a hand over the speaker. "Mr. Belmont wants to help me out. What should I do?"

"Let him, for God's sake!"

"You're sure?"

"Yes I'm sure! Tell him you'll take it!"

McGuffin smiled. "Later, when you remember this, and you will, be kind." Then he removed his hand from the speaker and asked, "When and where?"

"Shall we say lunch at one at my club?"

"We shall," McGuffin agreed, then listened to directions while Marilyn squeezed him and waited impatiently for a report.

Chapter 3

Victor Belmont's club, in the penthouse of a new black marble and smoked glass tower on Park Avenue, seemed rather modest for "probably the richest man in New York." True, the view of Central Park and much of the world was impressive, but the pool was scarcely Olympian, the exercise room could accommodate a couple of dozen at best, and the paneled dining room only a few more. It was only the cozy bar, with French windows open to a roof garden, with which McGuffin could find no fault. Its massive walnut bar, overhanging cabinets and beveled mirrors seemed ripped from a Victorian London pub by a great wind and deposited intact, along with the blazing hearth. In fact this wasn't too far from the truth, as the furnishings had been bought whole from a defunct pub in Leeds and flown over on the larger of Belmont's private jets. A muted plaid carpet had been added, along with a random selection of low pine tables and horse-hide chairs, until the effect, certainly after a brace of malt whiskeys, was more a place in the Scottish Highlands than the Manhattan skyline.

When, after touring the gardens with his host and returning to find no one in the bar except the uniformed help, McGuffin observed, "Your club must not have very many members."

Victor Belmont laughed "When I said, 'my club,' Mr. McGuffin, I meant just that," he said, indicating a barstool.

"The Belmont Athletic Club and Dining Hall has only one member, and that member is me."

McGuffin, who had vowed he wouldn't be knocked out by Belmont's wealth but was briefly staggered, replied, "Oh," as he climbed up on the barstool.

"I own the building," Belmont added, as he sprang up beside McGuffin. He was small but well conditioned, as befits a man with his own athletic club. Although close to fifty, his short curly hair was still thick and brown. The nose and chin were sharp in profile, the eyebrows thick and dark, but the most remarkable feature was the eyes. They were wide but inscrutable blue voids, dealmaker's eyes, eyes that while watching also listened, felt, smelled and tasted. "What would you like to drink, Mr. McGuffin?"

McGuffin said he would have a club soda, ignoring the expensive whiskeys the barman stepped aside to display. "I never drink when I'm on a case," he explained, when Belmont insisted he have one. This was true but misleading, as McGuffin's consumption between cases was the stuff of legend in San Francisco.

"But you haven't yet officially started," his potential client reminded him.

"In that case I'll have a Jameson's with a splash," McGuffin allowed.

"I'm afraid our only Irish whiskey is Bushmill's," the barman apologized.

McGuffin shook it off. "That's English whiskey."

"Give Mr. McGuffin a taste of my malt scotch," the host ordered. "Then get rid of the Orange whiskey and get in some Jameson's. I apologize for not having noticed, Mr. McGuffin."

"You're one of us?" McGuffin asked, dubious.

"I grew up in St. Ant'ony's Parish in Brooklyn," Belmont answered, the pear-shaped vowels replaced suddenly by the dialect of the streets. "Hell, I still vote Democrat."

"No shit?"

"No shit."

15

"And all this?" McGuffin asked, gesturing about. "You did it all by yourself?"

"Not entirely," Belmont answered. "My father, God rest his soul, was into buyin' and rehabin' and rentin' for a long time. Hell, he owned most of the neighborhood when he died, then it got gentrified and I was suddenly worth a couple of million. So then I started gettin' inta things, buyin' n' sellin' companies, puttin' up buildings, a little a this a little a that," he went on, swaying rhapsodically to the sweet beat of success, lapsing from the mellifluous locutions of Park Avenue to the harsh bray of Flatbush, like a Ferrari stripping gears.

"So although I may have been born with a silver spoon in my mouth, the gold and platinum I made myself," the entrepreneur went on.

Belmont only stopped talking when the barman placed their drinks on the bar. *My* malt scotch was just that, McGuffin realized when he saw Belmont's name prominently displayed on the label. The man drinks his own whiskey in his own club in his own skyscraper. The only thing in the place he doesn't own is me, McGuffin thought, as they saluted and drank.

McGuffin sighed, the scotch was that good, then said, "I take it I'm here because somebody tried to blow you away."

"Exactly."

"Who?"

"I have no idea."

McGuffin glanced skeptically at him, then said, "So tell me what you do know."

Victor Belmont pushed his drink aside and turned to McGuffin. "It happened at the family compound, upstate. My wife and I were asleep in the main house when the bomb went off, blowing up the car and part of the garage and setting the place on fire. That's how Johnny, my little brother, was hurt. He was sleeping in the guest cottage, just across the courtyard from the garage. He was awakened by a noise from the garage, got up to investigate and got as far as the courtyard when the bomb went off. That's when I jumped out of bed and ran to the window," he said, reaching across the bar for his glass.

McGuffin waited while he drank, then asked, "What did you see?"

"Fire," he answered. "One end of the garage was blown away, there were burning pieces everywhere—and Johnny. He was climbing to his feet, his robe was on fire. He ran across the yard and dived into the pool. Then I ran down and pulled him out and stayed with him until the ambulance came." He took another quick drink and turned back to McGuffin. "Thank God the pool was there. His burns turned out to be only minor."

"Too bad he was there at all," McGuffin added.

"One way or another, I'm going to see it never happens again," Victor Belmont vowed. "Will you help me "

McGuffin swirled the whiskey in his glass and stared at it for a moment before replying. "Don't think I'm not flattered, Mr. Belmont, but what makes you think I could be more effective than the police?"

"The attempt occurred upstate, not in Manhattan," Belmont informed him. "And even though the bomber happens to be a fellow New Yorker, the investigation is primarily the responsibility of the county sheriff's office, which, with all due respect, is not at all the same as the NYPD."

McGuffin nodded. "What do you know about the bomber?"

"Only what I read in the papers. He drove a cement truck, played pro ball at one time, left a wife and three young kids. He was obviously working for somebody else, but I have no idea who."

"Did your brother know this guy?"

"Angelo Tieri," Belmont supplied. "No, Johnny didn't know him."

"Did you ask?"

"I don't have to ask. Look, Mr. McGuffin, if you're going to take the case there's one thing you have to understand. My brother is a sweet kid, I practically raised him after our parents died. He loves me like a father and he wouldn't hurt

17

me for anything in the world. Now that's just something you have to take on faith, okay?"

McGuffin nodded. "Who should know better than you?"

"Fine," Victor Belmont said, clasping McGuffin on the shoulder. "Let's have lunch."

McGuffin slid off the stool and followed his host into the dining room. Its paneled walls were lined with Impressionists, millions of dollars worth. His wife, an ex-model, was a collector, Belmont explained, as if to dispel any notion that she was an empty-headed beauty.

They sat at opposite ends of a gleaming mahogany table set with monogrammed silver and china, and listened as the chef described his creations in a mix of French and English. McGuffin allowed Belmont to order for him, soup, salad, poached salmon and a white Bordeaux. The barman poured the wine as a pretty young woman in a short flared skirt wheeled out the soup.

"Delicious," McGuffin said, after the first taste.

"I stole the chef from the Tour d'Argent," Belmont said.

"You must give some wonderful dinner parties."

Belmont shook his head as he lifted his soup spoon. "He's only the lunch chef."

"Of course," McGuffin said. A lunch chef and a dinner chef, just like the orphanage where he grew up.

Over salad, the last course, and a second bottle of wine, Victor Belmont began to expound on his managerial style. "When you do business the way I do, you ruffle a lot of feathers. Some are hawks, some are chickens. I don't worry about the hawks, they're always up front. It's the chickens who hire the hawks who give me fits. You know what I mean?" he asked.

"Um, um-hm," McGuffin said, crunching an endive. In fact business puzzled him—how can you sell something you don't own?—and ornithology was hopelessly beyond him. The detective dealt with solid objects that didn't fly and he wished his client would soon return to them.

"That's not something you learn at the Harvard Business School, there's no call for it. Most of those wimps are going

18

directly into the corporate womb—keep your nose clean, work up to CEO and write a book nobody will read. That's not business, that's corporate welfare. Business is creating something where there was nothing, working without a net. Don't you agree?"

"I never use a net," McGuffin assured him, as he refilled his wineglass.

Belmont smiled, dabbed at his mouth with his napkin and inquired, "What's your fee?"

"Five hundred a day plus expenses," McGuffin lied.

"I'll double it, starting today."

"I haven't decided to take the case," McGuffin informed him.

"Oh? How much do you want?"

"It's not the money."

"Then what is it?"

"In my experience, when a well-planned attempt like this is made on a man's life, that man almost always knows who is behind it and why. And even at the risk of offending millions of law-abiding Italian-Americans as well as organized labor, when the bomber is an Italian-American Teamster, I have to think that the attempt on your life might be mob related. In short, Mr. Belmont, I don't think you're leveling with me."

"Um—yes, I see what you mean," Belmont mumbled. "And in your orbit I'm sure your experience is valid. But in mine I'm afraid it's not. It's a matter of numbers—people, events, velocity—hundreds of them, more than you can imagine. I buy and sell companies, and in the process make and break a lot of careers. I've offended a lot of powerful people, supported some politicians and seen to the defeat of others. I've attacked unions and management and a lot of people whose names I can't even remember. You want suspects, I'll give you a list as long as your arm."

At a thousand dollars a day—McGuffin calculated. He knew he should jump on it even though it didn't quite make sense. True, Victor Belmont's affairs were beyond his experience, but not Victor Belmont. How could a guy who'd

19

grown up at St. Ant'ony's in Brooklyn, unless it was terribly different from his own parochial school playground, not know when he'd picked on the wrong guy? Nor did McGuffin yet believe that a San Francisco PI was the right man for the job. There was one perk, however, that weighed heavily against any objection.

"You mentioned a lawyer—?" the detective reminded him.

Belmont nodded. "Andre Hersh, the best divorce lawyer in New York. If anybody can get your daughter for you, it's Andre."

"You foot the whole bill?"

"Every penny."

McGuffin plopped a spiral notebook on the table and removed a pen from his jacket. "Okay, let's round up the usual suspects."

Chapter 4

Sheriff Strock's office was in the basement of the red brick courthouse on the town square, guarded by a stout woman with a pencil sticking out of her gray bun. She was Mrs. McBride, the same genial Irishwoman who had assured McGuffin, before he had rented a car and driven up there, more than a hundred miles from the city, that the sheriff would be happy to see him. In fact she gave McGuffin the impression that since the bombing her boss had nothing much to do in this sleepy county besides entertain an occasional visitor from the city. He was therefore surprised when she rather brusquely informed him that the sheriff was unable to see him, but he could go over the file with Henry Dunkel, the property clerk, whose office was in the building across the square.

The property clerk, not even an investigating officer, McGuffin complained to no one as he crossed the grass to the squat limestone building where the records were kept. He found Henry Dunkel in the bowels of the building amid rows of mismatched filing cabinets, cartons filled to overflowing and tables piled high with papers and tagged debris. Henry, a skinny freckle-faced kid with lank brown hair that hung to his shoulders, grinned and climbed to his feet, a gesture resembling an opening stepladder, and ambled across the littered floor to the waiting detective.

"Mrs. McBride said to show you the Belmont file," he said, after introducing himself. He scratched his head, which was nearly a foot above McGuffin's, as he looked across the basement, presumably for the file, then flicked a bit of scalp from under his fingernail, narrowly missing McGuffin. "I had it out just the other day—" he murmured, while turning right and left like a windmill in an erratic breeze. "Ah!" he said, pointing a finger in the air, suddenly remembering. Then he lowered his head and started across the room, lifting each knee high in the air before slapping his long skinny foot on the cement. He disappeared behind a row of cabinets and, after a moment of clanking steel sounds, returned with a smudged manila folder, which he plopped on the counter in front of McGuffin.

"Sheriff was keeping this in *his* office 'cuz of all the newspeople coming around, but he finally got tired of that," Henry said, as McGuffin pulled papers from the file.

The uncorrected carbon was signed by a Lieutenant T. Dwyer, who was the first to arrive at the scene. The garage was on fire and an unidentified male was being attended to by two unidentified males, the terse official report informed him. In the next paragraph the parties were identified and in still a later paragraph Johnny Belmont was taken away in an ambulance.

"This doesn't tell me much," McGuffin said, waving the page at Henry. "Can I talk to Lieutenant Dwyer?"

"Not without the sheriff's okay," Henry answered.

"And I suppose that would be difficult."

"Unlikely. If you tell me what you want to know, maybe I can help."

"I'd like to talk to an eyewitness."

"That'd be like talkin' to a sack of teeth and bones, and one of the teeth wasn't even there. I assisted the coroner and the lab man the next day," he informed McGuffin, with some noticeable pride.

"Congratulations," McGuffin said, as he picked through the papers. There were signed statements from the servants, both Belmont brothers and Victor's wife, none of them at all illuminating. Johnny Belmont heard something, went to investigate and was knocked to the ground by an explosion.

22

Victor Belmont saw him a few moments later, robe afire, running for the pool.

"The scientific part, that's what I like," Henry went on as McGuffin read. "That's the only reason I took this job. I love to look at things and see things nobody else sees."

"Did you happen to see anything at the Belmonts' that no one else saw?" McGuffin asked without looking up.

"Exactly the opposite," he answered.

"Huh?"

"I *didn't* see something everybody else saw. But they didn't either. They only assume they did and that's good enough for them, but not for me. I have to see it before I'll believe it."

"You have to see what?"

"I'll tell you when I see it," he said, with a great grin that threatened to crack his freckles.

"Look, Henry, do you know something you're not telling me?"

"Not yet. But if I do I'll let you know."

"I'm panting to hear," McGuffin said. He slipped the statements back in the folder and handed them to the property clerk, then turned and started out.

"Where can I call you?"

"At the Gramercy Park Hotel," McGuffin replied, and was immediately sorry. He had a vision of this weird kid showing up one day and following him around like a crime groupie.

Angelo Tieri's apartment was situated between a Chinese fish market and an Italian hardware store in the Bensonhurst section of Brooklyn, directly over a funeral parlor. The street teemed with hungry people bound for one or the other of the several Italian restaurants in the area, while white-haired women watched from open windows behind fire escapes that zigzagged up the sides of the buildings like black lightning bolts.

McGuffin stepped out of a cab, edged his way across the sidewalk and into the doorway, located Tieri on the bank of buzzers and pushed. He was about to push the button a second time when a woman's voice crackled over the intercom, demanding to know who he was.

"Mr. McGuffin. It's about Mr. Tieri's insurance," he said.

"Insurance? You from the union?"

McGuffin hesitated briefly before replying yes. The buzzer sounded and he was in, walking down the paint-laden wainscotted hallway, dead fish to one side, humans to the other, then up the worn marble treads to the second floor, where a young woman with a baby on one hip waited.

Both the woman and her baby stared noncommittally while McGuffin expressed his sympathy and thanked her for seeing him. "I wouldn't bother you at such a difficult time if it wasn't important," he said, flashing his altar-boy smile.

"I already told the police and the insurance and everybody everything I know," she said in a weary voice. She had thick dark hair and equally dark circles under both eyes, but she was still quite beautiful, with a smooth olive complexion and large dark eyes. She wore a black, cleavage-revealing blouse tucked into a pair of well-fitted red slacks.

"I'll make it as quick and painless as possible," McGuffin promised.

She sighed audibly and stepped back, drawing McGuffin in and closing the door after him. He followed her to the kitchen and waited while she arranged the baby in his play-pen, then followed her into the dining room. All the signs of grief were there—faded framed photographs on every lace-covered surface. Parents and grandparents, uncles and aunts, scores of them, filling the room with silence. The dining table was arranged with bereavement cards and a black-shrouded chest of drawers had been made up as an altar, with candles in red glass and figures of the Virgin and the Sacred Heart. A photograph of a young man in a Chicago Cubs baseball uniform, smiling, determined, crouched to pounce on a ground ball, rested in the center of the altar.

"He got called up for a few weeks when they had some injuries," she responded to McGuffin's interest. "He played a few innings, then they sent him back down, so he finally quit."

"Good glove, weak bat," McGuffin said, quoting the obituary.

"Growing up in Brooklyn, he didn't see good pitching," Nina Tieri recited, while gazing at the picture. It had the ring of a familiar lament often heard round the table with uncles and nephews after a good dinner and a lot of wine. When the baby began to cry she went to the kitchen and lifted it out of the playpen. When she returned, the baby was quiet, staring curiously at the stranger in the house.

"I suppose you're gonna tell me you're denying coverage like the other guy 'cuz Ang was doin' somethin' illegal," she said, while bouncing the baby on her hip.

McGuffin shook his head. "I could never hit a curve ball myself, Mrs. Tieri. If I can do anything to help you, I will." The widow's expression softened faintly when McGuffin added, "He was a good-looking guy."

"Catcha the class," she said, followed by a smile that quickly disappeared. "Sometimes I think he was *too* good-looking."

"Too good-looking?" McGuffin questioned, although he understood. Angelo Tieri had the strong chiseled features of a movie star playing the role of a baseball player, as well as the lean hard body of the athlete. He was a man that, married or not, women would have a hard time staying away from. And judging from the accounts in the *Post*, Angelo Tieri did little to aid them in their resolve. "You mean he was bothered by women?"

"Angelo was never *bothered* by women," she said. "Everybody loved Ang, men and women both, they was always tryna do something for him."

"Who?"

"Guys."

"Mobsters?"

"You call Laird Strauss a mobster?" she challenged.

"Laird Strauss—" McGuffin repeated. He had heard the name. Then he remembered. Victor Belmont had placed it somewhere halfway down his list of suspects. He had been the biggest real estate developer in the city until Victor had switched from mergers and acquisitions to real estate. "Your husband was working for Laird Strauss when he was killed?" McGuffin asked.

"Not then, before. He worked for him for a coupla months."

"Doing what?"

"I don't know—drivin' him around, deliverin' stuff, whatever— "

"What kind of stuff? Did he say what he was delivering?"

She shook her head. "I doubt if Ang even knew, that was his trouble. If somebody said here's a hundred dollars, deliver this package for me, Ang u'd do it without even askin' what was in it. It could be cocaine and Ang u'd believe it was sugar."

"Or a bomb?"

"Sure, why not? Anybody knows Ang'll tell you, he'd never hurt nobody. If he was delivering a bomb, he didn't know what he was doing."

"I'm sure that Angelo wasn't *entirely* responsible for what happened, Mrs. Tieri," McGuffin began gently. "But we have to accept the fact that he did accidentally trip a bomb while trying to attach it to a car. He had to have known what he was doing."

"No, I figured that out," she said, hoisting the baby higher on her hip. "Somebody coulda told Ang they were just tryin' to scare Belmont by blowin' up his car."

"Who?"

She looked away and shook her head. "I wish I knew. 'Cuz if I knew who killed Ang, I swear, I'd kill the guy myself."

The thought of this hundred-pound Madonna blowing away a mobster was an unlikely one; almost as unlikely as her belief in his innocence. "Did Angelo come into any money shortly before he was killed?"

"No, nothin'."

Lying, McGuffin decided. "Did he know Victor Belmont?"

26

"Yeah, sure, we went to parties at his penthouse all the time," she scoffed.

"Then you have no idea who might have hired Angelo to plant that bomb?"

"Mr.— What's your name again?"

"McGuffin—Amos."

"There's something you gotta understand about me and Ang, Mr. McGuffin. This apartment's rent controlled and Ang made good money driving a cement truck, but when you got three kids you can always use a little more. And when Ang started bringing in a little more, I never asked where it was coming from 'cuz I didn't wanna know. And if I didn't wanna know about that, then I had no right to complain about the other stuff."

"What other stuff?"

"You know, the girls. Angelo was weak, people used to take advantage."

"What people?"

"You know—Conrad. He was always showing Ang the fast life—the huntin' lodge and the Poison Club. When I hollered, Ang just tol' me, 'I work for Conrad, I gotta play with Conrad.' "

"Conrad—?"

"Conrad Daniels,' she responded. "Hey, I thought you said you were from the union."

"The private investigator's union," McGuffin said. "I lied so I could talk to you, but I can help you," he quickly added.

"You aren't from any insurance?"

McGuffin shook his head. "I've been hired by Victor Belmont to find out who's trying to kill him."

"You're workin' for Victor Belmont and you wanna help me? What am I, some kind of an idiot? Get the hell out of here," she ordered, thrusting her chin in the direction of the door.

"Please listen, I can help."

"How? My old man's dead. How you gonna help me "

"By finding the man responsible for his death. You want

27

him and so does my client. If you help me find him you'll not only get revenge, you'll also get a nice reward from Victor Belmont," McGuffin promised.

"I want you outta here!" she ordered, as the baby suddenly began to wail. "Now see what you done!"

McGuffin waited while she soothed the baby and coaxed the bottle into its mouth. "He's a good-looking boy, like his father," McGuffin said.

"It's a girl," she snapped.

"Sorry."

"Three kids, all of them girls. It made Ang sick. The other two's with his sister."

"That's a help," McGuffin said, trying to hold his position. "I'm sure you've thought about the effect this could have on their lives—" he began.

"You mean like when her wedding's announced in the *Times*? 'Maria is the daughter of the late Angelo Tieri, who was blown up when trying to plant a bomb on a car'? No, I haven't been thinkin' too much about that as a matter a fact, because to tell you the truth I been too busy worrying about where her next meal is coming from."

"Then let me help," McGuffin pleaded. "My client is not your enemy. You both want to know who's responsible for Angelo's death, even if for different reasons."

"I can't help you!" she cried. "I can't tell you anything about Angelo's business 'cuz Angelo never told me!"

"Who's Conrad Daniels?"

"He's the jock sniffer from the union," she answered. "Ang made it to the majors, so in Conrad's book he was one of the boys. He used to take 'em all up to his hunting lodge once in a while and to his club—the Poison Club. That's not the real name of the place but the guys call it that 'cuz to their wives it's poison."

"What's the real name?" McGuffin asked, pulling the spiral notebook from his breast pocket.

"That's one of the things I didn't ask and Ang didn't offer. The same with the hunting lodge—I just know it's someplace up in the Adirondacks. The only thing I know is

28

Conrad's a big man in the Teamsters, so you don't wanna go lookin' for no trouble, if you know what I mean."

"Yeah, I know what you mean," McGuffin replied. "Have you spoken to him recently?"

"You kidding? Ever since this thing happened I'm like Typhoid Mary. Suddenly nobody wants nothing to do with me." As if she understood, the baby began to cry again. "Look, Mr. McGuffin, that's all I know, okay? Now you gotta go, you're upsettin' the kid. Please?"

"Okay," McGuffin said, allowing her to back him to the door.

It was all he was going to get from Nina Tieri right now, but he had the feeling she knew more and if he was patient he might get it. At the door he thanked her and wished her well and told her he would call when he had some information. She told him not to bother.

Chapter 5

Laird Strauss's tower was not as big as Victor Belmont's. What it lacked in size, however, was more than compensated for by its glitz. The lobby floor was a gleaming pink and onyx marble mosaic; the walls, except for the back, which was a two-story waterfall, were mirrors and gold; and the first-floor shops were filled with men and women with tanned faces in fur coats speaking foreign languages. McGuffin made his way through them to a man dressed apparently as a Swiss Guardsman, who directed him to the express elevator that would shoot him directly to the offices of the Strauss Realty Corporation on the top floor.

When the elevator doors closed and then opened only several moments later, McGuffin found himself under a large glass dome on the top floor. A beautiful receptionist who looked as if she bought her clothes downstairs sat at a glass table, smiling as if she expected him to buy a condominium. When the formalities were done, McGuffin informed her that he would like to see Laird Strauss.

"Do you have an appointment?" she asked through an unbroken smile.

"I'd like to buy a condominium," McGuffin replied with a matching smile.

"In that case let me get someone from our sales department," she said, reaching for the phone.

"This is rather a substantial purchase," McGuffin said,

placing a hand on the receiver. "On behalf of a client who requires the greatest discretion."

"All of our salespeople are extremely discreet," she assured him.

"My client insists I deal only with Mr. Strauss," he replied, continuing to press the phone down.

"I see," she said, taking her hand off the phone. "In that case, Mr. McGuffin, I would suggest you write a letter to Mr. Strauss's personal attention, telling him what you can about your client's needs, and I'm sure he'll get back to you."

"I'm sure we can do away with all that if you'll just pick up the phone and tell Mr. Strauss that my client is Mrs. Angelo Tieri," McGuffin said, handing her the receiver.

She sighed wearily and pointed to the wall of chairs across the room. "If you'll take a seat."

McGuffin did as directed and waited while she dialed, then spoke to someone, presumably Laird Strauss. McGuffin could hear nothing of the conversation other than "Tieri," which apparently evoked some reaction at the other end. The woman's eyes widened as she nodded and listened, then quickly hung up.

"I'm sorry, Mr. Strauss is not in his office," she informed him.

"Who were you talking to?" McGuffin demanded.

"His secretary."

"Where is he?"

"I'm sorry, I don't know."

"What kind of an organization is this " McGuffin asked. "I'm ready to spend several million dollars and you can't even tell me where Laird Strauss is? Maybe I'd better take my business to Victor Belmont."

"You're free to do that if you wish," she replied coolly.

McGuffin demanded her name, which she gave easily, then tried again to find out where her boss was hiding, but to no avail. After promising to invest his millions with Victor Belmont, McGuffin stalked across the room and took the elevator to the gleaming lobby.

31

"Have a nice day," the Swiss Guardsman said, as McGuffin walked past him.

"Yeah, you too," McGuffin snarled, then stopped suddenly and turned. "Damn, I forgot!"

"Sir—?" the Guardsman inquired.

"Laird Strauss. His secretary told me where I was to meet him and I've forgotten." Muttering over the loss of youth, McGuffin started for the elevator, stopped suddenly again and turned. "You wouldn't happen to know the name of the place, would you?"

"The place—?" the Guardsman asked uncertainly. "All I know is, tonight's the night Mr. Strauss is giving his big yacht party."

"Of course!" McGuffin said, slapping his thigh. "I'm to meet him on his yacht, the, the—"

"The *Enterprise*."

"Exactly! Which is docked out at—"

"*Down* at," the Guardsman corrected.

"Down at—?"

"The Twenty-third Street Pier."

"Of course!" McGuffin exclaimed. "And what time does the party begin?"

"The boat leaves at seven, I believe."

"I think you're right," McGuffin said, passing a twenty-dollar bill to the Guardsman, who swallowed it up with the discreet efficiency of the tip mongerer.

McGuffin fairly danced across the lobby and out onto Third Avenue to a waiting cab. He was beginning to feel the rhythm of the city.

Black limousines rolled to the berthed yacht in a steady procession, disgorging men in dark suits and pencil-thin women in fur coats who hurried up the gangplank and into the salon. To McGuffin, standing inconspicuously near the stern as the sun was setting over the Palisades, this could as easily pass for a nautical funeral as a power party. None of the celebrants he recognized, including the mayor, a couple of film stars, a boxer and a Jets quarterback, seemed all that

32

happy at the prospect of spending the evening circling Manhattan Island aboard Laird Strauss's yacht.

McGuffin waited until a crowd had collected at the gangplank, then moved quickly along the boat and slipped in among them. He smiled familiarly and chatted inanely to the middle-aged woman ahead of him as they climbed up the gangplank to where a large uniformed officer greeted each guest by name. There was a loud silence when McGuffin stepped aboard.

"This is my first time—Mr. McGuffin?"

It didn't register. "May I see your invitation, Mr. McGuffin?"

"I must have left it in my other suit," McGuffin said, patting himself down.

When McGuffin smiled conspiratorially—you know how absentminded we society types can be—the officer smiled back, amused. For judging from the baggy flannels, here was a gatecrasher who only owned one suit. "Journalist?" the officer guessed.

"Private investigator," McGuffin answered, seeing the game was up. "I just want to ask Mr. Strauss a few questions."

"Sorry, you'll have to phone the office for an appointment," he said, firmly grasping McGuffin's elbow.

"I did, his secretary told me to see him here," McGuffin lied. When he tried to pull free, the officer's grip tightened. "You must tie a good knot, sailor," McGuffin observed.

"I wasn't hired for my nautical skills," the bodyguard said, smiling easily at the guests filing past. "Now, are you going down the gangplank or over the side?"

"Do me a favor, just tell your boss it's about Angelo Tieri," McGuffin pleaded. "What have you got to lose?"

"My job. Let's go," he ordered, easing McGuffin gently but inexorably toward the gangplank.

McGuffin took a step backward then slammed himself noisily against the bulkhead and shouted, "Oww, you've broken my back!" alerting the last knot of guests at the salon door.

"Okay, we'll do it the hard way," the bouncer said, raising a fist.

33

"Before this goes any farther, you should know I'm a black belt in karate," McGuffin warned, speaking quickly. "So unless you want to be badly embarrassed in front of all these people, I'd advise you to drop that hand and go get your boss. Right now—ooh!"

It wasn't the right hand poised in front of his face that got McGuffin, but an unseen left to the solar plexus that sent him sliding down the bulkhead to the deck where he lay in great pain, gasping uselessly for air while slowly turning the color of his imaginary karate belt. McGuffin flopped about the deck like a landed fish, striving frantically to summon air to his collapsed lungs, until at last the oxygen came on wheezy legs and he was pulled roughly to his feet. He heard his name and his occupation mentioned, and caught a bleary-eyed view of a stout man in a black officer's cap and matching blazer, glowing with gold buttons and braid. He might have passed for an overweight U-boat commander with a lopsided nose, had McGuffin not first viewed a photograph of the subject of his pursuit, Laird Strauss.

"Unnecessary roughness," McGuffin complained in a strangled voice. "I just want to—talk to you about—Angelo Tieri," he gasped.

Laird Strauss looked closely at McGuffin's pale bleary eyes, as if to file the face away in his mind, then asked, "Who are you working for?"

"That's confidential," McGuffin answered.

"Get him off my boat," Strauss ordered his bodyguard.

"You're making a mistake!" McGuffin called, as the large bodyguard pulled him away. "You employed the man who tried to kill Victor Belmont! And you're going to have to answer! Either to me or the police!" he shouted this last as he was thrust off the gangplank, a five-foot jump that sprawled him flat on the pier. A pant leg was torn and blood was oozing from a scraped knee, he saw, as he climbed to his feet. Even at a thousand dollars a day, this was not an expense he was willing to bear.

"And you're also gonna pay for this suit!" McGuffin shouted, as he limped after the departing yacht.

Laird Strauss stood clutching the rail, glaring malevo-
lently at the limping detective as his yacht glided slowly
down the slip, leaving the frustrated McGuffin finally at the
end of the pier, hurling useless threats into the darkening
air. Then when the ship turned downriver and the band
began to play, Laird Strauss turned away from the man on
the pier and walked to the salon. His concerned expression
changed to a pleased smile when he stepped through the
hatch and saw his rich successful friends beaming happily at
him.

The next day McGuffin bought two new suits, a sports
jacket and a pair of pants, all of them, except for the pants,
brown. He had intended to limp up to Brooks Brothers on
his tender knees in the hope of finding a pair of gray flannel
pants to replace his torn ones, until the savvy bellman had
pulled him aside and given him some sage advice.

"Only suckers pay retail," he said.

He then gave McGuffin the names and addresses of several wholesale establishments where an entire suit could be
had for the cost of a pair of pants at a fancy uptown joint.
McGuffin was doubtful, but because most of the places were
only a few blocks away on lower Fifth Avenue, he decided
to try one of them. To get to it he had to take a freight
elevator to the ninth floor and walk up to the tenth floor
where he found thousands of suits hanging from floor to
ceiling on bare pipes in an otherwise empty loft. An old
man wearing a tape measure around his neck admitted him
through the steel cage and asked how he tore his pants.

"I fell off a boat," McGuffin said, as he was led through a
forest of clothing.

"He fell in the water and he tore his pants," the clothier
remarked, as he stuck one hand into the hanging suits.
"From here to the end is forty-two, you want gray I got
plenty."

McGuffin browsed through the suits, selected a brown
tweed and tried the coat on. It looked and felt like a million
dollars—five hundred anyway. "How much?" he asked.

"A hundred and fifty, including alterations. And for you I'll add knee pads so you shouldn't go falling in the water and tear your pants."

"I'll take it," McGuffin said.

When he learned there'd be no tax if he paid cash, McGuffin selected another suit and a sports jacket, in varying shades of brown, and a pair of gray flannel pants that matched his suit coat as long as he stayed out of bright light. Then with his purchases under his arm, the on-site alterations completed, the gleeful detective hobbled back to the Gramercy Park Hotel, where he tipped the bellman twenty dollars.

"By the way, there's a Mr. Belmont been callin' you like crazy," Eddie, the bellman, informed him as he pocketed the twenty.

"Thanks," McGuffin said.

"That wouldn't be Victor Belmont, would it?" Eddie asked with a smile that winked.

"It would," McGuffin answered.

Eddie's smile fell a couple of inches. "You're workin' for Victor Belmont and you're buyin' cut-rate suits?" he asked, plainly disillusioned.

Feeling suddenly insecure, McGuffin clutched his purchases to his chest and walked across the lobby to the elevators. Once safely in his room, he spread the cut-rate clothes out on the bed and compared them to the Brooks Brother suit. Nobody could tell the difference, he assured himself, after viewing each jacket in the mirror, Still, he knew he would not rest until his new clothes were passed by a more qualified judge. He was wondering who that might be—Marilyn perhaps—when the phone rang. It was Victor Belmont.

"Is it true, did Laird Strauss have to throw you off his boat last night?" he demanded.

"Not Strauss, his spring," McGuffin corrected. "A great big guy." It was embarrassing enough being tossed off a boat without his client thinking it was at the hands of a

36

deskbound real estate developer. "How did you hear about it?"

"He phoned me this morning, that's how I heard about it!" Belmont shouted. "He's pissed, McGuffin; he's threatening to sue me! Will you tell me why the hell you told him you were working for me?"

"I didn't, he just assumed it," McGuffin answered.

"I told you this job required an anonymous detective and what do I get? I get a shamus who busts up Laird Strauss's yacht party."

"I'm sorry," McGuffin said. "All I can say is, it seemed like the right thing to do at the time. I mentioned Angelo Tieri's name and it got me nothing."

"And why the hell should it?"

"I talked to Angelo's widow. She told me he worked for Strauss—I want an explanation."

"Tieri worked for Strauss?" Belmont repeated in a suddenly softened tone.

"That's right."

"Doing what?"

"Chauffeur, delivery—She claims she doesn't know much about Angelo's activities and I tend to believe her, up to a point. And if Strauss employed Angelo to do nothing more than that, there's no reason he shouldn't talk to me. But if he hired Angelo to wire a bomb to your car, it's perfectly understandable why he wouldn't want to discuss it, especially with your private investigator."

"I see," the chastened client replied thoughtfully.

"If I can establish a connection between Laird Strauss and Angelo Tieri through someone besides Tieri's wife, I'm sure it'll get the district attorney's interest," McGuffin promised.

There was a silence followed by "I think I know somebody who might be able to help.

"Who?"

"His name is Conrad Daniels."

"The union guy?" McGuffin asked, as Nina Tieri's warning leapt to mind: "You don't wanna go lookin' for no trouble."

37

"You know Conrad Daniels?"

Victor Belmont laughed shortly. "Anybody in the construction business knows Conrad Daniels. He's the man who sees there's no labor trouble on the job."

"You mean he's a bag man."

"Is that any way to talk over the phone?" he replied. "Be in front of your hotel in fifteen minutes, I'll tell you the whole story."

McGuffin said he would and Belmont abruptly clicked off.

Fifteen minutes later, dressed in his new brown tweeds, McGuffin was standing in front of his hotel in the early-afternoon sunshine, drawing mental diagrams among Laird Strauss, Conrad Daniels, and Angelo Tieri, when Victor Belmont's limousine came to a stop at the curb. Belmont opened the door ahead of the driver and motioned to McGuffin with an Italian wave. The car was in motion before McGuffin had pulled the door closed.

"Where are we going?" he asked, when the driver turned down Fifth Avenue.

"To the battlefield," Belmont answered.

McGuffin nodded, sat back in the seat and waited for an explanation. At a thousand dollars a day he could afford to be patient. They turned right on Fourteenth Street and made their way across town, past stores spilling out onto the sidewalk with cheap goods, then turned and sped south down the broad West Side Highway.

"What did you hear about Conrad Daniels?" Belmont asked, as they flashed by Christopher Street.

"Only what Tieri's widow told me, that he's some kind of union boss who likes athletes. And because Angelo had been a major leaguer, Daniels apparently used to see that he was always taken care of."

Belmont nodded, apparently satisfied, then added, "It's a passion he shares with Laird Strauss. Strauss has always got a horse or a fighter going someplace or other. None of them ever seems to win. I told him he should try putting the

38

horses in the ring and the fighters on the track. That was when he was still talking to me," he said, as he picked up the intercom. They were in sight of a modern building constructed on landfill on the bank of the Hudson, connected to another building by a covered overpass across the highway. He ordered the driver to pull off the highway onto a narrow strip of gravel where he parked at the foot of a great pyramid of sand. He instructed the driver to wait, then motioned for McGuffin to follow him out of the car.

Belmont pulled a tan cashmere polo coat over his shoulders and walked toward the river while McGuffin followed, wearing only his tweed suit. The fall wind blowing down the river from Canada was a chilly portent of things to come. Near the edge of the river, Victor Belmont stopped and whirled around, planted his feet wide apart and pointed up at the lower Manhattan skyline.

"The tail end of Manhattan, the part that wags the economic dog. Down there," he said, pointing to the new building extending over the highway, "is the world headquarters of American Express. And over there is Wall Street and over here is Battery Park City. And you know what this is, right here where we're standing?" McGuffin didn't. "I call it Striped Bass City," he said, and laughed.

"This is the battleground, Amos," he said after recovering. "This thin strip of river bottom is where I met and defeated Laird Strauss. When I decided to move into Manhattan real estate, nobody gave me a chance against Strauss. And for a while it looked like they were right. It seemed that every time I went after a choice parcel, Strauss beat me. Or if I won, it turned out not to be as valuable as I thought. For the longest time I couldn't figure out how to beat him, but finally I found his weak spot. And do you know what it is?"

"Striped bass?"

Belmont smiled. "Close. Laird Strauss is a gambler. And all gamblers, Amos, are losers. They have streaks, but eventually they lose. So all I had to do was induce Strauss to bet heavily on an apparent sure thing, then make sure that it wasn't. I had to get Laird Strauss to bet his ass on a fish.

"This fish," he said, stamping the ground. "Striped Bass City. When the West Side Highway project was announced, I let it be known that I intended to buy this strip of property, then fill in the river and build the grandest building in the world. It was going to be a mixed business-residential building designed by a team of distinguished architects. It was going to be the international headquarters of several of the world's largest corporations, with the most luxurious apartments in New York, each with its own swimming pool and boat slip. There would be schools and stores and gyms and theaters; there would be a helicopter port and several hydroplanes speeding residents up and down the river, and even an enclosed all-season summer park. That was my dream, Amos. What do you think of it?"

"It sounds like a nice addition to the neighborhood."

"And that's exactly what Laird Strauss must have thought too. Because the next thing I know he had topped my bid on the property by several million dollars. Several million, Amos, for a strip of land that was hardly wide enough for a bowling alley. So I upped him several million more and called a press conference. I announced that I was betting my entire fortune on this project and dared Laird Strauss to compete with me. And then," he said, grinning, "the game was afoot."

"You won," McGuffin surmised.

"No, I lost," he replied, still grinning. "Strauss got it, for the highest price ever paid for Manhattan realty. He paid a thousand times what it was worth because he was a gambler. He gambled that the West Side Highway would be completed and that he would be allowed to fill in the Hudson River. And ten years ago it looked like a sure thing."

"Then what happened?" McGuffin asked, looking around at the still-bare strip of land.

"Neither of those things ever happened. The highway plan was defeated and the landfill permit was denied when it was discovered it would destroy the striped bass."

"So Strauss owns this property and he can't do anything with it," McGuffin concluded.

40

The developer shook his head. "I bought it from him last year. For considerably less than he paid, naturally."

"Why, if you can't build on it?" McGuffin asked.

"For sentimental reasons, I guess. And of course there's always the chance the environmentalists might have a change of heart," he added.

"Of course," McGuffin said. No doubt the latter had far more to do with his decision than sentiment. "So you managed to tie up most of Strauss's capital for the last ten years, while you were becoming king of the island."

"I do believe you have a flair for real estate, Amos," his employer remarked.

"And I can understand why Laird Strauss might want to kill you. But why," McGuffin asked, "would he wait almost ten years to do it?"

"Strauss couldn't blame me when the highway failed to go through, or when his landfill permit was denied. Nor could he blame me when he finally sold this property to the Striped Bass Corporation for five cents on the dollar. But," he said, pointing a finger in the air, "when he found out that I and the Striped Bass Corporation are one and the same, then I think he might have become a little peeved."

"That would seem to explain it," McGuffin agreed.

And if Daniels had a chance to throw something somebody's way, why not to Angelo Tieri, a good glove man? However, if Daniels had been the one to put Laird Strauss in touch with Angelo Tieri, it wasn't very likely that he was going to want to talk about it with Victor Belmont's private investigator. There was also, McGuffin realized, an even graver reason Conrad Daniels might not wish to talk to him.

"Before I come down on Strauss, there's something I have to know about you and Conrad Daniels," McGuffin said.

"What's that?"

"Is there any possibility that Daniels might be the one who sent Angelo Tieri after you?"

The idea struck Victor as extremely funny. He laughed,

then replied, "I'm sure Conrad has no wish to kill the goose that lays the golden egg."

"Okay, it's Laird Strauss," McGuffin said. "Now how do I get to Conrad Daniels?"

"I'll see what I can do," he promised. He pulled the polo coat around his neck, then glanced up the river in the direction of the offending wind. "It's getting cold," he said. McGuffin nodded and followed.

When they got to the car, Belmont stepped back and appraised the detective. "New suit?" he asked.

"Yeah," McGuffin replied, then stood, waiting for a reaction.

Victor Belmont climbed into the car without another word, followed a moment later by the insecure detective.

Chapter 6

Victor Belmont phoned McGuffin the next day to inform him that Conrad Daniels would meet with him at seven that evening in his apartment, an elegant prewar building on Park Avenue. To the rest of America *prewar* connotes the depression, while to New Yorkers it suggests sprawling apartments with manned elevators, oak paneling and soundproof walls, the sort of apartment favored by bankers, lawyers and stockbrokers, not cigar-chomping mobsters in cheap striped suits. But McGuffin was in for still another surprise when he saw Conrad Daniels standing in the living room with his wife, a thin blonde with lots of teeth, surrounded by several well-dressed teens.

Daniels separated himself from the photogenic group as the maid led McGuffin in, and walked across the room with a broad smile and an open hand. He was trim as a jockey, wearing a blue cardigan over his shirt and tie, sharply pressed tan slacks and tasseled loafers. His summer tan was still fresh and the only hint of his age, which McGuffin put at about forty, was a dramatic streak of white hair from the front of his tightly crinkled pompadour to the back.

He greeted McGuffin warmly, then pulled him into the room and introduced him to his wife and son as well as each of his prep school friends, all of them as polished and friendly as their hosts. The whole group in their tweeds and flannels, posed among the English antiques and dark oils that hung from the moldings in gilded frames, resembled

43

more a Ralph Lauren advertisement than the portrait of a mobster at home.

"Gilbert and his staff have just put the school paper to bed so their father is springing for dinner at Dorrian's," Anne Daniels said, while clinging warmly to McGuffin's hand. She wore a plaid skirt and sweater with two strings of large pearls and spoke with a faint British accent, an unlikely moll.

"I wagered they wouldn't publish the first edition before Thanksgiving—it usually comes out after Christmas—but wouldn't you know, this year they were on time," Conrad Daniels said, giving his son a proud, one-armed hug.

"You deserve it. He'll bet on anything," Anne Daniels said to McGuffin.

"It was a reach but we made it," Gilbert said.

When his father released him, Gilbert herded his staff of journalists, four boys and three girls, to the door. They all thanked Mr. Daniels for dinner, politely acknowledged McGuffin and Mrs. Daniels and left.

"Nice kids," McGuffin remarked after they had gone. Nina Tieri and Victor Belmont were either the poorest judges of character in New York, or he was in the wrong apartment.

"They're such sweet kids, all of them," Mrs. Daniels affirmed with a dreamy smile. She had the hollow cheeks of a famine victim but the ravenous teeth of a piranha. She clasped her hands and turned to McGuffin. "I'm terribly embarrassed, Mr. McGuffin, but I can't quite place you. Was it the library benefit last month?" McGuffin shook his head. "Jackie's party in Southampton?"

"Mr. McGuffin is a detective, dear," her husband interrupted.

"Oh," she said, the smile draining from her face. "I'll leave you to your business," she said, backing away, then turning and disappearing into the labyrinthine bowels of the vast apartment.

Daniels offered the detective a drink, which he refused, then indicated one of two couches flanking the fireplace.

44

"Very nice place," McGuffin observed, once they were seated on opposing couches.

"You can't beat the old buildings," Daniels said, delicately plucking at his sharp creases. McGuffin thanked him for taking the time to talk to him and Daniels assured him he would be only too glad to help if he could. "I just can't imagine anyone having it in for Vic. That man has done more for this city than anyone since Moses."

"Moses—?"

"Robert Moses? Oh, I forgot, you're from San Francisco, aren't you? Wonderful town." McGuffin smiled. He had always thought of it as a city. "I must say, I was rather surprised when Vic told me he had hired a San Francisco investigator."

"Me too," McGuffin replied.

"So tell me, what can I do to help?"

"You can tell me about the bomber," McGuffin said. "I understand Angelo Tieri was a good friend of yours."

"I admired him," Daniels allowed. "If you'd ever seen him play shortstop you'd know what I'm talking about. Reminded me of Rizzuto—in the films, I mean. But I wouldn't say we were close friends."

"But you drank with him at the Poison Club."

Conrad Daniels pursed his lips and shook his head. "I'm sorry, I don't know the place."

"That's not the real name, of course. The actual name is—what is it?" McGuffin asked, snapping his fingers.

"I have no idea."

"It's not important. I just thought he might have dropped something after a couple of drinks that might suggest who he was working for."

"I'm afraid not. Angelo and I were scarcely what you would call drinking buddies."

"Not even at your hunting lodge?"

"My hunting lodge?" Daniels asked, with a puzzled look. "Where did you hear this?"

"From Angelo's widow," McGuffin answered.

"Ah, of course," he said, the puzzle solved. "I'm sure

45

she's still in shock. I don't own a hunting lodge and I've never heard of the Poison Club. She's obviously thinking of someone else."

"Obviously," McGuffin said. "She did seem a bit distraught—no money—no help from the union. Do you know Mrs. Tieri?" he asked.

"I've met her."

"Do you think you might be able to talk to someone in your union about helping—?" he asked.

"My union?" Daniels interrupted.

"You are an official in the Teamsters Union, aren't you?"

"I'm an attorney, Mr. McGuffin. A labor relations attorney. I have represented the Teamsters from time to time, but that's the extent of my relationship."

"I see," McGuffin said. Suddenly it was clear, the apartment, the antiques, the Ralph Lauren family. Conrad Daniels wasn't a mobster, he was a mob lawyer, an ombudsman, a respectable middleman between business and the labor bosses. He negotiated the bribes and sent guys like Angelo Tieri to collect. He was the insulator between briber and bribee, the guy who saw that nobody got burned, for which he was rewarded with all the trappings of genteel success. Daniels wasn't a liar, he was simply a fastidious observer of the meaning of language and the law.

"I understood that you functioned as a liaison between labor and the construction industry, but I didn't know it was legal. I mean that you were a lawyer," McGuffin added, with an ingenuous smile.

"Yes, I'm a lawyer."

"And Angelo Tieri was your paralegal?"

Daniels laughed easily, unoffended. "Angelo was good with the glove, not the books. Angelo worked for the union, usually as a job steward, never for me."

"But he did perform some services for you once in a while?"

"I tried to throw things his way whenever I could."

"Such as?"

"Various and sundry errands."

46

"I see," McGuffin replied. "Did you ever recommend him to Laird Strauss?"

"Laird—?" he asked, staring thoughtfully past the detective. "I might have, I can't remember," he said, focusing back on McGuffin. "Why? Surely you don't think Laird tried to kill Vic, do you?"

"Victor Belmont beat Strauss out of millions of dollars on his West Side Highway project," McGuffin informed him. "People have been known to kill over a hell of a lot less than that."

"But not Laird Strauss," Daniels replied. "Laird's a player. He likes to win, but more important, he knows how to lose."

"Then why won't he talk to me?" McGuffin challenged.

"You asked him about this?"

McGuffin said he had and proceeded to tell the lawyer about being eighty-sixed from Laird Strauss's yacht on the evening of his party.

"Perhaps your timing was bad," Daniels suggested.

"I don't think Strauss is anxious to talk to me at any time."

"Nonsense. If you'd like to talk to Laird, I think I can arrange it. Although I'm sure you're wasting your time," he warned.

"I'll take that chance, if you're willing to set up a meeting," McGuffin assured him.

"Do you have a number where I can reach you?" the lawyer asked, glancing at his Rolex. The interview was done.

McGuffin scribbled his name and number then tore the sheet from his notebook. Both men got to their feet and met halfway between the couches. Daniels glanced at the paper, stuffed it into his cardigan pocket and led the detective to the door.

"By the way, I will speak to someone at the union about Mrs. Tieri," he remembered, when he got to the vestibule. "Although I'm only a legal representative," he added, as he stopped at the door and turned to McGuffin.

47

"I'm sure she'll appreciate whatever you can do," McGuffin said, shaking hands. "And thanks for your help."

"I'm only too glad to do anything I can to help Vic. We're very good friends, you know."

"So I understand. Victor suggested that much of his success is due to your . . . labor management skills."

"I try to keep everybody happy," the lawyer replied.

"I imagine that requires a bit of juggling at times."

"Delicate negotiations," he corrected.

"And are all your clients happy with these negotiations?"

"They're every bit as happy as I am," Daniels assured him. "Victor Belmont's death would be great loss to all of us," he added, as Mrs. Daniels entered and looked around the room.

"Oh, there you are," she said, finding them in the vestibule. "Don't forget, dear, we have the AIDS thing tonight."

"I hadn't forgotten, darling," he assured her.

"So nice to have met you," she said, flashing a wincelike smile at McGuffin before speeding from the room.

"You too," McGuffin said, as her husband opened the door for him. He led McGuffin across the foyer to the elevator, pressed the button and turned to the detective.

"I don't profess to know much about your business, Mr. McGuffin, but isn't it usual to ask who stands to gain the most by the victim's death?"

"You mean his brother?"

"And partner," Daniels reminded him. "I'm not accusing Johnny of anything, you understand, but it seems you'd want to talk to the man who stands to inherit one-half the Belmont Organization in the event of his brother's death."

"You're right, of course," McGuffin said. "But Victor thinks his little brother is above suspicion."

"I can understand that," Daniels said. "I used to think Johnny was okay too, until I heard some talk."

"What kind of talk?"

Daniels frowned and spoke slowly. "Johnny built an enormous house up at the family compound, all concrete."

"Yeah?"

48

"And he signed the material off to one of his brother's projects."

"Where did you hear this?"

"Like I said, it's talk. Vic knows the contractor, he can check it out for himself if he wants to."

"Did you mention this to Victor?"

"Not me," he said, shaking his head. "I know how Vic feels about the kid—it's off with the messenger's head. I figure if it's just a little family embezzlement, why get involved? But after somebody tried to kill Vic, I begin to wonder if maybe Johnny might be capable of something a lot more serious than just stealing. You see what I mean?"

"Yeah, I see what you mean," McGuffin said. "Do you know of any connection between Johnny Belmont and Angelo Tieri?"

Again the lawyer frowned, as if the pain had returned. "There was some talk."

"What kind of talk?"

"Johnny was asking around for a guy."

"A bomber?" McGuffin pressed.

"I don't know the details. According to the talk, Johnny's bookmaker was leaning on him and he wanted somebody to get him off."

"Who did you hear this from?"

"I don't remember."

"This could be very important," McGuffin urged.

"Look, Mr. McGuffin, you have to understand, the people I work with don't approve of people talking about this sort of thing, even though it might not impact directly on them, and I've already told you a lot more than I intended. Now do what you want with it, but do me a favor, forget where you got it."

"I'll do what I can," McGuffin answered, as the elevator doors slid open, revealing a smiling uniformed attendant.

"And I'll do what I can for Mrs. Tieri," Conrad promised as the doors closed.

Chapter 7

The walls of Andre Hersh's Park Avenue law offices were covered with photographs of happily smiling divorcées, some of them famous, all of them wealthy. Some were posed drinking champagne with their lawyer, some hugging or kissing him, while other pictures showed a woman alone, posed against the spoils of marital war—a prewar apartment, a country house or an entire business. One showed a well-developed young woman in a bikini waving from the stern of a yacht named *Nick and Sabrina*, with a line through Nick's name.

"Sabrina wasn't my brightest client," Andre Hersh said, noting McGuffin's interest. "Her old man was in the saloon business, a cash business, had to be knocking at least a quarter of a mil off the old income tax return. A guy in that position isn't exactly dealing from strength, I'm sure you know what I mean. I could have gotten her at least half the business but she opted for the toys—the Hatteras, the Porsche and the house in East Hampton. Small change. She lacked heart, Mr. McGuffin. I tell them coming in, divorce is a mean and dirty business, you got to get down. Show me an agreeable divorce and I'll show you a lawyer who isn't doing his job. Any woman who's getting married, I tell her, you're not prepared to rip your husband's throat out, you're not prepared to get married. But what am I telling you, a private detective, a man of the world," he said, settling his short round body into a tall leather chair.

He smoothed the lapels of his pinstripe jacket, chosen for the illusion of height, tugged at his tie, then felt to be sure that the last few remaining strands of hair were still artfully arranged over his shiny pate. It was a nervous drill with which McGuffin was already familiar, like a batter preparing to hit. He grunted as he pulled his chair closer to the desk, then swiveled to face his client.

"I usually don't take male clients, I'm strictly offense, but thanks to Victor you're getting the best, Mr. McGuffin, the very best. Have a chair."

McGuffin assured him of his gratitude and sat gingerly on the French antique beside the desk.

"I like to play offense but I can play defense when we lose the ball. Only with me the best defense is a good offense, to quote Woody Hayes. I like to see grown men broken and weeping, not women. Only for you and Victor I'll make an exception."

McGuffin assured the lawyer that he had no wish to see Marilyn broken and weeping. "I just want to take Hillary back to San Francisco, as the custody decree provides."

"Yeah, the custody decree," the lawyer said, as a troubled frown crossed his face. "I know this might come as a shock to you, Mr. McGuffin, you being a man of the law, but that custody decree is only printed on paper, not carved in stone. And even though your ex moved your daughter out of California without the court's permission, that still doesn't mean the court's going to order your ex to bring her back."

"Why not?" McGuffin demanded. "She's in violation of a court order."

"Circumstances change, Mr. McGuffin. Courts recognize this. For instance, if the mother gets a job in another state, the court will almost always allow her to take the child and go."

"But she didn't get a job. She's paying Franz Tutin more for acting lessons than she can ever make. And it's mostly my money," McGuffin complained.

"Nevertheless she's advancing her career, apparently without any harm to her daughter."

"Are you telling me the New York public school system isn't harmful?" McGuffin demanded.

"I'm a product of the New York public school system," the lawyer answered, pointing to the law degree crowded among the smiling divorcées. "And that's hardly an argument a New York court is going to sympathize with. By the way, may I offer you a drink?"

"Is the news that bad?"

"Not necessarily."

"No thanks, just tell me where I stand."

"You're fucked."

"No—"

"Given the facts. But facts, like the law, can always be changed, to liberally paraphrase Blackstone."

"What do you mean?"

"If your ex moved to New York not to pursue a career in the legitimate theater but to lead a life of willful and wanton depravity among drugged, sex-crazed actors, without regard for the well-being of her impressionable minor daughter, then we might have reason to return Hillary not only to California, but also to your sole keeping."

"No, no," McGuffin said, shaking his head. "I don't want to take Hillary away from her mother, I just don't want her taken three thousand miles away from me."

"Understood," the lawyer said, catapulting himself forward in his chair with such force that it seemed he might be propelled across the room and splattered all over his divorcées, until at the last minute he grabbed the edge of his desk and held. "Now you must understand that for me to accomplish this, you've got to get mean. You've got to tear her throat out, leave her broken and weeping. Because if you're not willing to do that, Mr. McGuffin, justice will not be achieved."

"I can't do that," McGuffin replied. "I don't know what you have in mind, but I'm not ready to destroy Marilyn in order to get Hillary back."

"I speak metaphorically, of course," Hersh said, releasing

the desk. "All we do is put your ex in a position where she can clearly see the worst possible scenario, namely the loss of custody of her child, and from there we negotiate."

"And how are we going to do that?" McGuffin asked. "Marilyn doesn't do drugs, at least not anymore, she's not a drinker and she doesn't even have a boyfriend."

"It's easy," he said, opening and spreading his hands. "We hire a private investigator."

"A PI? You mean frame her?"

"Mr. McGuffin, I'm surprised at you. Surely a man in your profession should be the last to leap to such a conclusion," the lawyer said, wide-eyed and innocent. "I merely propose that we hire an investigator to conduct a fair and impartial investigation of the subject's habits. If it turns out that her life is a model of decorum, that'll be the end of it. I'll submit a modest bill to Victor and I'll advise that you return to San Francisco without incurring any further useless legal expense, and of course without your daughter. But if on the other hand he should turn up anything that might reasonably be construed by the court as reason to remove your daughter from the custody of her mother, then we shall mention that fact to your ex in our subsequent negotiations."

"You can jerk yourself around all you want, but I'm not going to be a party to any fabrication of evidence," McGuffin said, climbing to his feet.

"Who's to know the evidence is fabricated?" the lawyer asked, turning his innocent face up to his client.

"Marilyn will know," McGuffin replied. "And if she thinks I'm trying to get Hillary back on some trumped-up charges, she'll— I just don't want it that way."

"But how will she know that you know the charge is trumped up? Or for that matter, how will you know? Don't you see, Amos, I and my investigator are your insulators. All you've done is come to me for legal assistance. How I conduct my investigation and negotiations are my responsibility. If my investigator's report is flimsy, or heaven forbid false, she won't capitulate—her lawyer will see to that. But if there's anything to it at all, then I'm sure we'll find

53

Marilyn a bit more sympathetic to your rightful paternal concerns. Again, her lawyer will see to this."

"She doesn't even have a lawyer," McGuffin pointed out. How could he take advantage of anyone so innocent?

"She soon will, don't worry," Hersh assured him. "But that doesn't mean we'll have to go to court and throw a lot of dirty laundry around. Trust me, Amos. I'll get your daughter back to San Francisco and Marilyn will never know she's been through the ringer."

McGuffin knew better. For although all men might be equal before the law, their lawyers were not. And Andre Hersh was the best money could buy. He was going to rip Marilyn's throat out and leave her broken, weeping and childless. And McGuffin couldn't allow that.

But on the other hand, who am I to spare Marilyn, as well as my conscience, at Hillary's expense? McGuffin asked himself. Sure, I can decline Hersh's assistance and leave Hillary to these mean streets, but would that be acting in her best interest—even though it's what Hillary wants? Or should I do everything in my power, much as I hate to do it, to see that Hillary enjoys a normal childhood in San Francisco whether she likes it or not?

It was a difficult choice, but in the end McGuffin was up to it.

"Rip her throat out," he instructed his attorney.

Chapter 8

This time, preceded by an introduction from Conrad Daniels, McGuffin was received by Laird Strauss in his penthouse office, albeit grudgingly. "I want you to know I'm doing this as a favor to Conrad," Strauss informed him, once they were seated behind the closed door in his office. "I don't know who tried to kill Victor and I couldn't care less."

"It seems to me that if Victor beat you out of millions of dollars, you might care very much to see him dead," McGuffin suggested.

"Why, would that get me my money back?"

"Vengeance is its own reward."

"Not to me, I'm a businessman. So state yours and let me get back to it."

"Let me start by correcting the record—you know very well who tried to kill Victor."

"What—!" he exclaimed, bolting out of his chair.

"Or do you deny that Angelo Tieri worked for you?"

"Oh, that," he said, sitting back down. "I thought we were talking about who's behind it."

"Maybe we are."

"I don't take insinuation lightly, McGuffin, not even from a friend of Conrad Daniels," the developer warned, pointing a finger at McGuffin's head. "Who told you Angelo worked for me?"

"Conrad."

"I don't believe you."

"Why not?"

"Because that's not his style. With the kind of people Conrad does business, you learn to keep your mouth shut or you get whacked. You've been talking to Angelo's widow and don't bother denying it because I know. Sure I gave him a job, but I didn't hire him to kill anybody. Conrad told me to put him on the payroll, so I did, it's that simple."

"Not to me," McGuffin said.

"Then let me spell it out," he said, as if to a child. "Conrad Daniels has me and every other builder in this town by the balls. We do what he says or nothing gets built. And if that means hiring a shortstop, fine, it's better than hiring a whole goddamned team."

"If you hadn't hired Angelo and you refused to be intimidated by the threat of a strike, do you think he'd kill you?"

Laird Strauss stared incredulously at McGuffin for a moment before asking "Where are you from?"

"California."

"What, don't you get the newspapers out there?"

"Do you think Conrad could have ordered Victor's execution?"

"Sure, he could have. But why? People like Victor and me, we're the guys who keep Conrad in business. No, if I was looking for the guy who tried to kill Victor, I'd look for the guy who stood to *gain* the most by his death, not *lose* the most."

"Some people might say that was you," McGuffin suggested.

"Only if they didn't know anything about the inheritance laws," he replied.

"His brother?"

"Who else?"

"But Johnny Belmont is already a very wealthy man," McGuffin pointed out.

"And if Victor should die, he'd be twice as wealthy."

"But I understand the brothers are very close, more like father and son."

"And gold is thicker than blood."

56

"Do you know Johnny Belmont?"

"I see him around."

"Do you think he's the kind who could murder his brother?"

"Maybe not," Strauss said. "But he knows how to delegate authority."

"Angelo Tieri—?"

"It makes sense to me."

"Do you know of any connection between Angelo and Johnny Belmont?"

"No, but I wouldn't be surprised. Johnny's a sportsman, likes to hang out with jocks. True, Angelo was small potatoes, Johnny prefers the Mantles and the Namaths, but it's possible."

"Have you heard anything about Johnny's new house?"

"Only that it cost a fortune."

McGuffin pressed, but Strauss seemed to know nothing of any embezzlement. Then he asked about Johnny's gambling.

"He bets big, very big, that's all I know."

"Do you know his bookmaker?"

"Probably Gregory Scott, the society bookie," he replied after a moment.

"A society bookie?"

"He claims he went to Yale or someplace, I don't know. You want to talk to him, try the sports bars, Jimmy's, Rose's, the Dona Bella."

"Thanks," McGuffin said, entering the names on a blank page of his notebook. "Is Gregory Scott the kind who might resort to violence to collect a debt?"

"Now why would Gregory Scott kill Victor in order to collect from Johnny?"

McGuffin didn't answer. Blowing up Victor, or even his chauffeur, might be an effective way to let Johnny know that his debt was seriously overdue. It was also possible that the bomb was meant not for Victor's car but for Johnny's— but only if the bookmaker had run completely out of patience. The society bookmaker wasn't a likely suspect, McGuffin had to admit, when the interview with Laird

57

Strauss came to a close a few minutes later. But it didn't matter, he had another.

Strauss was of course right about Conrad Daniels—mobsters don't gossip. Yet Daniels had freely volunteered that Johnny Belmont was an embezzler, was in debt to his book and had been looking around for a bomber. Conrad Daniels is either in violation of the mob code, or for some reason he would like me to believe that Johnny Belmont tried to kill his brother, McGuffin decided as he stepped out into Laird Strauss's gold and marble foyer.

Chapter 9

An hour later, with a pastrami on rye still laying heavily on his stomach, McGuffin lay on his bed, "Sherlocking" about the case at hand. At a thousand dollars a day plus expenses, the Belmont case was probably the best he would ever have, as well as the most frustrating. The principal difference between New Yorkers and Californians seems to be accessibility, McGuffin decided. Everybody here comes with their own fortress. Even if I do find out who tried to kill Victor, the district attorney won't be able to get in to arrest him. And Johnny Belmont, my prime suspect, has been placed off limits by my client. The situation is impossible. I know I should just take the money and shut up, but I can't.

And I'm going to tell him, McGuffin decided, sitting up and throwing his feet on the floor. You can fire me, fire my divorce lawyer, do anything you want, but I'm not doing another thing until I talk to your brother, he rehearsed silently as he reached for the phone.

"I'm sorry, Mr. Belmont is not in," his secretary informed him.

"Where is he?" McGuffin demanded.

"In Hell's Kitchen with the mayor," she answered, and gave him an address in the west Forties.

McGuffin thanked her and hurried downstairs to a waiting cab. He had heard about the mean streets of Hell's Kitchen and the Irish gangs that roamed them, but until he drove by the old stone church that housed the Actors Company, he didn't realize that he had passed this way before. Just around the corner the driver turned down a street bordered by derelict cars and decaying tenements and stopped behind a pair of displaced limousines. McGuffin paid and stepped out of the cab only a moment before the driver raced away. A large group, mostly black and Hispanic, was assembled on the walk near the limousines where Belmont and the mayor should be. But as McGuffin approached he saw no sign of either of them. Many of the buildings were boarded up, while several with Rent Strike signs in the windows were apparently occupied, probably by some of the people gathered around the limousines, staring at the approaching white man in the brown tweed suit.

"I'm looking for Mr. Belmont," McGuffin said.

"You work for Mr. Belmont?" a tall black man in a Yankee jacket asked, separating himself from the crowd.

"In a way," the detective answered.

"What way?" the Yankee fan asked, taking his large hands out of his jacket. "You the man lets the junkies and the winos have these buildings?"

"Not me," the McGuffin said, shaking his head.

"You the man busts the boilers so the pipes freeze? The man who set the fires in those buildings?" he said, pointing a long finger over McGuffin's head.

McGuffin continued to shake his head. "That's not my line of work, I'm just a detective looking for Mr. Belmont."

"Detective," he repeated. "You one of the guys bust in and wreck the apartment when the tenants go out?"

"Forget I asked," McGuffin said.

"You workin' for scum, mister, you know that? This was a good block, good people, till Belmont start buyin' buildings and trashin' 'em," he charged, following as McGuffin backed away.

"Look, I don't know anything about this, I just arrived in town from California," McGuffin protested. "But I intend to ask him about it if you'll tell me where he is."

"California? The man say he come from California," the

60

block leader said, turning to his amused constituents. They might be losing their houses, but not their sense of humor.

When he saw Victor Belmont emerge from a tenement, followed by the mayor and his entourage, McGuffin excused himself and pushed through the block association.

"You wanna ask Mr. Belmont, you can ask him now!" the black man called.

McGuffin started for the limousine while Belmont and the mayor, deep in negotiations, moved forward in starts and stops. McGuffin removed a hand from his pocket and started to raise it in Belmont's direction, when suddenly from behind a hand clamped down on his wrist and he was slammed facedown across the trunk of the limousine.

"Spread 'em!" his assailant shouted.

Relieved to know it was a cop, McGuffin did as directed. "Take it easy, I'm a private working for Victor Belmont," McGuffin informed the cop as he patted him down.

Then he heard Victor Belmont's voice—"Amos?"—and the cop stepped away.

"Yeah, it's me," McGuffin said, straightening and turning to the cop. He wore a chauffeur's uniform but that didn't change anything. He was a cop, McGuffin knew, retired but still a cop, with a thick neck sticking out of a tight collar and mean blue eyes glaring out of a red Irish face.

"He's all right, Sean," Belmont said.

"Yes sir," Sean snapped, then retired to the other side of the car.

"Who's your spring?" McGuffin asked, dusting himself off.

"My new bodyguard," Belmont said, as they were joined by the mayor. Belmont introduced them and they shook hands. The mayor made no mention of the fact that a citizen had just been slammed across a car—this was New York.

"I've hired Mr. McGuffin to find out who's trying to blow me up," Belmont informed the mayor.

"What's the matter, you got no confidence in our state cops?" the mayor asked in a high thin voice. "If it had happened in the city we'd have him in jail by now. Let that be a lesson to you, Victor, never live anyplace but Noo Yawk. It's a jungle up there in the sticks—bugs, Lyme disease, bombs—you never know what. You're sure I can't buy you lunch? I know, I know, lunch is for wimps, but what can I tell you, I gotta eat. So long, Victor. You'll think about what I said. Nice to meet you, Mr. McGovern!" the mayor called, as he waved and stepped into his limousine.

As the mayor's car pulled away, Victor Belmont turned to McGuffin and asked, "How did you find me?"

"Your secretary told me you were here."

"Yeah, but Hell's Kitchen," he said, gesturing grandly at the squalor that surrounded them, seemingly amused.

"We've got slums in San Francisco," McGuffin replied. He'd show his client he was no hick.

Belmont laughed. "We'll make a New Yorker out of you yet, Amos. Come on, let's get in the car," he said, steering McGuffin to the limousine.

"Hey, yo!" the block leader in the Yankee jacket called. "You askin' the man about that shit?"

"I'm asking," McGuffin replied, as he slid into the limousine.

"Where are you headed?" Belmont asked, when Sean was behind the wheel.

"I came to talk," McGuffin answered. "But if Sean feels like driving, he can take me back to the Gramercy Park Hotel."

McGuffin settled back in the leather seat while Sean pulled away slowly from the block association, which had gathered around the car. The limousine had two phones and a facsimile machine, but no television or bar.

"Sam Ruggles was one smart real estate developer," Belmont said, as he gazed at the passing tenements.

"Who?" McGuffin asked. He didn't remember the name from the suspect list.

"The man who developed Gramercy Park after the Revolutionary War. He was able to sell the lots for ten times what they were worth, and do you know why?" McGuffin didn't. "Because with each lot the buyer got a gold key to the park. An iron key would have worked just as well, but Sam knew what the suckers wanted and he gave it to them. That's genius," he said. "How do you like the Gramercy Park Hotel?"

"Very nice."

"Maybe I'll buy it and give you a rate," he said. It was hard to tell if he was joking. "Now what did you want to talk about?"

"This investigation. It's tough enough working in a strange city, but I can't do it with one hand tied behind my back," McGuffin complained.

"Nor do I like to think I've hired a one-armed detective," Belmont replied. "Who's tied your hand behind your back?"

"You have."

"Me? What are you talking about?"

"Your brother. You tell me he's only an innocent witness, but he is a witness. He has information that could be vital to this investigation, but you won't let me talk to him."

Belmont smiled and shook his head. "Amos, believe me, Johnny knows nothing more than what I've told you."

"Let me talk to him," McGuffin pleaded. "Sometimes a witness can recollect more than he thinks he knows, if the interview is handled correctly."

"And I don't doubt you're very skilled at that," Belmont allowed. "But what can Johnny know except that there was an explosion? Or are you suggesting something else?"

McGuffin sighed audibly. "I'm not suggesting that your brother had anything to do with that bomb, or Angelo Tieri, or that he's anything other than what you say he is. But something might have happened prior to the event, something that Johnny is aware of but hasn't mentioned, only because it hasn't occurred to him that it might be relevant."

"Such as?"

"Such as an encounter with someone who might have been a little too curious about you—your schedule, the identification of your car—something that might have seemed entirely innocent at the time, but not in retrospect. All I want to do with Johnny is go back over events, to see if he

63

might see something differently now, in the light of what's happened since."

Belmont smiled patiently and explained it once more for the detective. "Until the bombing episode my life was an open book. Anybody who wanted to kill me could have easily managed without going to my brother or anybody else. And my brother has suffered a great shock, Amos."

"I appreciate that."

"Suggesting to him that he might have been even inadvertently responsible for the attempt on my life might very well cause him serious psychological damage, to go along with his physical injuries."

McGuffin sighed for a second time. He had exhausted his store of gentle persuasion; it was time for the ultimatum that would either end the most profitable investigation of his career, or perhaps bring it to a conclusion, however unwelcome to his client. "Do you know that your brother charged his new house to the company?"

From the expression on Victor Belmont's face, it was plain that he didn't. "Where did you hear that?"

"From an informant who prefers to remain nameless. His name isn't important, you can confirm it with the contractor who built Johnny's house."

"I'll do just that," Victor Belmont said, his expression hardening in a way the detective had not yet seen.

"And if it's true?"

"If it's true, you'll have my permission to take your investigation anywhere it leads you."

"Agreed," McGuffin said, offering Victor his hand.

"But I can't believe such a thing of Johnny," he added with a limp handclasp.

McGuffin released his hand, settled back in the soft seat and looked out the window, away from his client. They were inching down Ninth Avenue, locked in Lincoln Tunnel traffic, past open food stands swelling out onto the sidewalk. Deer and wild boar hung in one window, pheasants and wild ducks in another, rabbits and squirrels in still another, while common beef and fish were everywhere.

64

"There's something else I have to ask you," McGuffin said.

"Yes?"

"That guy in the Yankee jacket told me you were a block buster. He said you put junkies in some of your buildings and set fire to others. Is that true?"

Victor Belmont turned a sad face to his detective. "That's about as far from the truth as you can get. That block has been deteriorating for years, for reasons all the sociologists at Columbia can't fully explain. The only thing everybody can be reasonably sure of is that I had nothing to do with it because I have nothing to gain by it. That's the kind of property my old man used to deal with, but not me, no more," he said, slipping gears. "The only reason I was there today is because the mayor wants my help. I don't know if I can take on a project like that, but if I do, do you know how much money I'll make?"

"I'm a stranger here," McGuffin answered.

"Not a penny, strictly pro bono. And if you see your friend again you can tell him I told the mayor I wouldn't touch his project unless every tenant on the block is satisfactorily relocated. Does that clear that up?"

"I just thought I'd ask," the chastized detective replied.

There was a message from Marilyn waiting at the desk. Fearing the worst, he stuffed the paper in his pocket and went to his room to return her call. His fear was justified.

"Amos, you bastard, you went out and got a lawyer!" she charged.

"Not exactly—" McGuffin stalled.

"What do you mean, not exactly? I'm holding a letter in my hand from an Andre Hersh advising me that he's been hired to represent you!"

"But I didn't hire him, Victor Belmont did," McGuffin pointed out. "Remember when I said 'Later when you remember this, be kind?'"

"Yes, but—"

"Well, be kind because that's what I was talking about.

65

Part of my compensation from Victor Belmont is a free lawyer."

"You're a prick, Amos. And you can be sure of one thing—I'll never allow my daughter to live in San Francisco with a prick. If you can get a lawyer, I can get a lawyer," she assured him, then slammed the receiver down.

McGuffin replaced the phone and sat staring uncertainly at it for a moment, wondering if his ex-wife was over-matched after all. Andre Hersh was an able lawyer, but Marilyn McGuffin, when aroused, was a formidable woman.

Chapter 10

The closest thing to the autumn hills of Westchester was a forest fire without smoke, the Californian decided, as he glided down a gentle twisting slope of the Taconic Parkway. At the bottom of the hill lay a long narrow reservoir glinting icily in the sun between bright red, yellow, and orange hills. There was little evidence of suburbia here, just the occasional village, usually marked by a white church spire sticking up out of the fall leaves. It seemed a much too serene and bucolic setting for an urban investigator, a place where game poaching and fishing out of season were the crimes of choice, not car bombs and embezzlement.

The directions to the Belmont family compound, unmarked anywhere except on the back of an engraved invitation that Victor had provided him, were unerring, despite several turns on ever-narrowing country roads. Prying the directions from Victor Belmont's hand, the last obstacle to this journey, had been a difficult task. Not even the contractor's admission that Johnny had indeed requested that the work to his house be charged to one of Victor's jobs was enough to convince Victor that his little brother was an embezzler.

"If he did it there was a good reason; there has to be an explanation," Victor had insisted as he finally handed over the directions.

The last stretch was a gravel lane through thick forest, opening finally on to a great stone house at the edge of a lake. It was a two-story English country house with leaded glass windows set deeply in stone and several tall chimneys poking out above the steeply pitched roof. A cobblestone drive spoked off the gravel circle between the main house and a smaller one, leading to the bomb- and fire-damaged garages beyond. There was a red Ferrari parked in front of the smaller house to the left and a station wagon parked around back.

McGuffin parked beside the Ferrari, got out and peered at the garage at the top of the cobblestone drive. The door and much of one wall had been blown away, exposing the burned-out remnant of a once-grand Mercedes limousine lying among the charred beams and boards of the garages. Of the several garages, which had apparently once been stables, only the two on the right end had been damaged.

He walked to the front door of the smaller house, his feet crunching noisily on the gravel, rang the bell and waited. The door was opened by a young woman in a starched nurse's uniform who, after McGuffin introduced himself, assured him that Mr. Belmont was expecting him and asked him to follow her. She had the kind of legs that could inspire a sick man to get well soon, McGuffin noted as he followed her into the living room.

The walls were paneled with rich carved wood and the fireplace was nearly as large as McGuffin's hotel room, but the room was almost bare of furniture. The dining room too had the look of bachelor pad, with only a few mismatched chairs grouped around one end of an enormous scarred dining table.

He found Johnny Belmont in the library cum bedroom overlooking the blown-out garages, seated in a leather chair in his robe and slippers. McGuffin told him not to get up but he did, stiffly, and shook McGuffin's hand. There was an unmade bed against the empty bookshelves at one end of the room, a television and VCR on a stand in the center of the room, a couch and chairs, and great piles of popular magazines everywhere. There were several photographs of Johnny and his toys on one wall, including one of him behind the wheel of the Ferrari out front and a glass case filled with hunting rifles and shotguns. Johnny introduced McGuffin to Nancy, who smiled hospitably and offered him a chair. Then she helped Johnny into his chair, holding his hand a beat longer than necessary, while warning him to be careful. When Johnny thanked her and suggested that Mr. McGuffin might like coffee, she leapt to the task, over McGuffin's polite protest.

"Wonderful nurse," McGuffin commented, when she left the room.

"But not much of a housekeeper," Johnny said, gesturing at the mess around them. "We've begun moving things to the new house but we're not yet settled in one place or the other." McGuffin assured him he needn't apologize, then asked about his burns. "The doctor says it's coming along fine, I just have to watch out for infection. That's why I've got Nancy," he added with a grin.

Another toy for the rich boy, guaranteed germ free. Victor Belmont might have the brains in the family, but his little brother was plainly the beauty. He had the same strong features as his brother, but he was taller by almost a head, with the boyish openness of a rich kid who didn't know the meaning of denial. His hair was light brown, almost blond, short and wavy, in keeping with the athletic, ruddy outdoorsman he so plainly was, and his eyes were as clear as the lake behind him, fairly twinkling with an eagerness for whatever adventure one might propose.

"Actually Victor's a lot more excited about it than we are," Johnny said. "My wife prefers the city and the guest cottage has always been good enough for me, but Victor thought we needed a showplace to entertain. So I hired a Bauhaus architect and built a James Bond house across the bay. If you'd like to walk down to the dock we can have a look at it," he offered, already squirming out of his chair. McGuffin protested but Johnny assured him that exercise was what he needed.

"You say the new house was Victor's idea," McGuffin prompted, as they started down the flagstone path to the lake.

"He was the instigator, Penny and I took it from there."

69

"Penny—?"

"My wife," Johnny replied. "You've never seen the *Penny's From New York* show on TV?" McGuffin said he hadn't. "I thought everybody knew it. Anyway, Penny's a Manhattan maven, knows everybody. Our job, Penny's and mine, is to entertain all the right people while Victor takes them aside to make deals, which is the reason for the house. We get the bankers and the investors up here for a little golf and tennis, take 'em out on the lake in the boat, give 'em a good dinner and shake a little more money out of them," he said, flashing the smile that made him indispensable to the Belmont Organization. "It's not much, but when you've got a brother who's a financial genius there's not much more that needs doing."

"I take it you think a lot of your brother."

Johnny stepped up onto the dock, then stopped and turned to the detective. "Vic's like a father to me," he said, then turned and walked on to the gleaming mahogany sailboat at the end of the dock.

"Nice boat," McGuffin said. Although they were not a passion—he did not enjoy being pitched and tossed about in confined spaces—this was a beautiful antique.

"I prefer the speedboat," Johnny said, pointing to the back of the bay.

McGuffin's eyes traveled across the water to the big speedboat at rest in a cavernous concrete boathouse, then climbed up the side of the hill where the house cantilevered out like a series of irregular stone steps, graced by balustrades and decks and walls of smoked glass. It was indeed a house fit for Bond, with room to moor a submarine in the boathouse below and to land a helicopter on the roof above. But the ultimate achievement of the architect, who had been ably assisted by God, was the stream from the cliff above the house that tumbled down from platform to platform in a controlled fall, finally to the roof of the boathouse where it slid in a shimmering sheet into the lake.

"The waterfall presented some serious engineering problems, but Vic wanted a showplace so he got it," Johnny said.

"I heard a lot of concrete went into that house," McGuffin said, as he continued to stare at the ponderous structure jutting out at all angles from the side of the hill.

"Quite a bit," Johnny said, before turning curiously to the detective and inquiring "You heard it from who?"

"Conrad."

"Conrad Daniels?"

"Yeah, you know him?"

Johnny nodded. "He and my brother do business together, sort of."

"Your brother told me all about it," McGuffin assured him. "Do you think Conrad might have sent Angelo Tieri up here to blow him away?"

"Hardly," Johnny answered. "If my brother was candid about his relationship with Daniels, I'm sure you can understand that Vic is the last man in the world Conrad would like to lose."

"The goose that lays the golden egg."

"Exactly. Shall we go up and get our coffee?"

McGuffin followed Johnny along the dock and up the path, thinking. It was true that Conrad wouldn't kill Victor if it meant the end of his protection business. But if killing Victor would make him Johnny's partner, then Conrad might be quite willing to give up the protection business.

When they reached the courtyard, McGuffin halted under the chestnut tree for a closer look at the scene of the explosion. One blackened hinge still remained attached to the charred post where the door had stood at the side of the garage. The swimming pool behind the main house was little more than a hundred feet from there, yet to the flaming man it must have seemed like miles. He looked back at the cottage door where Johnny stood waiting, then continued across the courtyard.

Nancy was waiting in the bedroom with the coffee when they returned, their empty cups on the table between the two leather chairs. When they were seated, she filled the cups and again left the room.

"I suppose your wife is too busy in the city to stay up here while you're recuperating," McGuffin observed.

71

"Penny stayed for a few days after I got out of the hospital, but that's about all the country she can take."

"Was she here on the night of the accident?" McGuffin asked.

"I was here alone," he answered. "I often come up here alone, just to unwind." From what? McGuffin wondered, but didn't ask. "I was in bed but not asleep, just lying here staring out this window, when I heard a noise—"

"You were awake at three-thirty in the morning?" McGuffin interrupted.

"I guess I hadn't yet unwound," he answered. "Anyway it was the middle of the night, too late for Vic or any of the help to be out there, so I went to investigate."

"You didn't call the police?" Belmont shook his head. "Or take a gun?"

"We don't expect those kinds of problems up here."

"Apparently Angelo was counting on that. Then what happened?"

"I started for the garage and the bomb went off. I found myself on the ground, my robe on fire, then I got up and ran for the pool. The next thing I knew, Victor and the chauffeur were pulling me out and I was on my way to the hospital. And that's all I know."

McGuffin nodded, then lifted his cup. "What kind of car do you drive?" he asked.

"That red Ferrari you saw in front of the house."

"Do you also have a sedan?"

"Yeah, a black Mercedes."

"Was your car in the garage on the night of the bombing?"

"Yes."

"Then it's possible that Angelo Tieri might have placed the bomb on the wrong car."

"That's ridiculous," Johnny scoffed. "Vic's car was a limousine, mine's a sedan."

"Rather a subtle distinction to a man bent on homicide," McGuffin suggested.

"You wouldn't say that if you had seen Victor's limousine," Johnny said. "Besides, I don't have any enemies."

72

"You like to gamble," McGuffin stated.

"I love it, but what's that—?"

"Are you in trouble with the bookies?"

"Of course not," Johnny replied, faintly indignant. "I only bet what I can afford to lose."

"Then you're not a real gambler," McGuffin said. "Real gamblers like to bet more than they can afford to lose—whether it's the rent on the tenement or the whole damn farm. And I'll lay ten to one you're a real gambler, Johnny. The kind who has to go to his friends to cover his losses—or to his brother."

"Did Victor tell you that?" Johnny demanded.

"Your brother bailed you out time after time, but this time he said no. This time you had to bail yourself out, but you couldn't, so your bookie sent Angelo Tieri to blow you up. That's what happened, isn't it, Johnny?"

"No," Johnny replied. "I owe a little money, but not enough so they'd send somebody to kill me. That's not the way they operate."

"Not the way who operates? Who do you owe money to?" McGuffin demanded.

"It's none of your business."

"Gregory Scott?" Johnny's look of surprise was the answer. "How much do you owe? A hundred thousand?"

"No."

"Two—?"

"It's nothing like that, it's nothing I can't handle," he insisted, clear blue eyes flashing anger.

"You're in sound financial shape?"

"Yes, I am. Not that that's any of your business either."

"Then why did you pay for your house with company funds?" McGuffin challenged.

Johnny opened his mouth to speak, but it took a moment for the words to follow. "Where did you hear that?"

"Do you deny it?"

"Of course I deny it, it's preposterous. And what difference does it make anyway? Who are you working for, my brother or the IRS?"

73

"Then it's true, you did embezzle funds from the company," McGuffin charged.

"Embezzle! How dare you accuse me of such a thing?" he shouted, leaping to his feet.

"That's what it's called," McGuffin said, prepared to duck.

"How can I embezzle money from my own company, huh? Tell me that!" he demanded, looming, fists clenched, over the seated detective.

"It's half your brother's," McGuffin pointed out, calm before the storm.

"Don't you think I know that? Do you think I'd pay for my house with company funds without him knowing about it?"

"Victor didn't know anything about it until I told him."

"You're a liar!" he shouted, and raised a fist.

"Johnny, taking a swing at me is not going to solve your problem," McGuffin advised. "In fact, it could make it a lot worse."

Slowly Johnny unclenched his fist and sat back down in his chair. "Sorry, but a man doesn't like to be called a thief," he said with a pouting look. "Victor told me to charge the cement work to one of his projects. After all, the house was to be used for corporate entertaining."

"Johnny, your brother told me that he did not authorize that payment. That's why I'm here. Now what the hell is going on? Who's lying, you or my client?"

"You've got it wrong, you must have it wrong," Johnny insisted. "Victor told me things were gonna be a little tight for a while, that he had to reorganize the corporation. Penny and I wouldn't be seeing as much money as we had, but it didn't matter, we'd be getting it in other ways. The house was supposed to be one of those ways. It was a trade-off, dividends for the house. I realize I might be in violation of the tax laws, but I'm not an embezzler. I only did what my brother told me to do."

"Tell me about this corporate reorganization," McGuffin said.

Johnny sighed and leaned back, wincing slightly at the pain. "I really don't know all that much about the business," he began. "Except that we were getting into some risky ventures and Victor was worried that the company might lose a lot of money—we might even become bankrupt. I told him it was okay, I trusted him, I'd do whatever he wanted me to do. But Vic was worried. He wanted to be a big player but he didn't think he had the right to risk my half of the company, so he came up with a reorganization plan that would protect me in case we went bankrupt."

"The Belmont Organization is in danger of bankruptcy?" McGuffin asked.

"We were leveraged, what do I know? Victor said reorganize, so I agreed."

"What kind of reorganization?"

"All my common shares, fifty percent, were converted to preferred. That way, in case of bankruptcy, I'd be paid off first. I told my brother I didn't want any preferential treatment, but he insisted on it."

"Did he tell you that preferred shares can't be voted?" McGuffin asked.

"Vic made all the decisions anyway," Johnny answered with a shrug. "I didn't think it mattered one way or the other—until my dividend checks stopped coming. Vic told me it couldn't be helped, it was a temporary constriction or something like that, and I'd have to get by on Penny's salary for a while. I told him I thought he should be able to shake a little money free each month anyway, but he said he couldn't."

"And that's when you learned you had no more voice in the running of the company," McGuffin surmised. Johnny nodded. "So you started gambling heavily to make up the shortfall."

Johnny stiffened, about to protest, then slumped back down. "Yeah, I bet a little more than I should. I'm into my book for about a hundred."

McGuffin was sure it was much more, but decided not to press it. A hundred thousand was more than enough to get blown away over. "So you went to Victor and asked for money to pay off your gambling debts, but he refused."

"He said he didn't have it, things were tight. I told him that between the construction costs and the no-dividend policy, I couldn't make it, I had to have more money. So that's when he told me to charge the cement work to the company. And I can't understand why he'd tell you anything different."

Neither did McGuffin, but he'd clear it up. One thing, however, was suddenly clear as the blue lake at the bottom of the hill—Johnny Belmont was a man with money problems, which his brother's death might conveniently resolve. And bookmakers tend to be in touch with the sort of person who can arrange just such an event. "I'd like to talk to your bookmaker," McGuffin said, reaching into his breast pocket for a notebook.

"Forget it," Johnny said. "I've got enough trouble with him without sending a private investigator around."

"If that's the way you want it," McGuffin said, returning the notebook to his pocket. "But if I was in your position, I wouldn't hold anything back."

"What do you mean?" Johnny demanded.

"I mean that you and Angelo Tieri were the only two people here when he tried to blow your brother away. You tell me that you like to come up here by yourself and unwind, but you're a playboy, you don't go anywhere alone. You're only here now to establish a pattern after the fact—and even then you have to bring your girlfriend along."

"So what?" Johnny asked. "I like girls. And you're right, when I come up here I usually bring someone along, but it's always a girl, never a guy. Or if it's a guy, he's never a bomber."

"Who was it that night, Nancy?" McGuffin asked, jerking a thumb in the direction of the door.

Johnny smiled and shook his head. "Nancy's new. That night I was here with my mistress."

It was McGuffin's turn to smile at this antiquated expression. Yet for a man such as Johnny Belmont, who could buy women just as he did Ferraris, the expression was perhaps apt. "What's her name?" McGuffin asked, again going for his notebook.

"This is just between us?" McGuffin nodded. "Her name is Antonia Ruiz. She was with me on the night of the accident and she'll verify everything I've told you."

"Where can I get in touch with her?"

"I'll take you to the club where she works." Johnny asked the detective where he could be reached and McGuffin wrote his name and number in the notebook, then tore off the sheet and handed it to him. On the next page he wrote Antonia Ruiz followed by a question mark.

"Why didn't you mention Antonia to the police?"

"To spare my wife."

"You're very thoughtful."

"I try to be."

"If Antonia's a put-up job, I'll know it," McGuffin warned, as he again returned the notebook to his pocket. "So if you're lying, tell me now and save us both a lot of trouble."

"She was right in that bed," he said.

"I hope so," McGuffin said, then climbed to his feet, followed by his host. He thanked Johnny for his information, shook his hand and started for the door.

"One last question," he said, stopping and turning at the door.

"Yeah—?"

"Did you know Angelo Tieri?"

"No."

"Never met him?"

"I said no, didn't I!"

"Just asking," McGuffin said. No reason to get so excited, he said to himself as he turned and walked out.

Speeding along the Taconic Parkway at sixty miles per hour, with the overture to Stravinsky's Firebird blasting out of the speakers and the autumn leaves blowing in the wind, McGuffin tried to find a reason for Johnny Belmont's innocence. There were several compelling reasons for his guilt, and they all came down to money. After the corporate reorganization that Victor had neglected to mention, Johnny found himself suddenly without money just when he needed it most—to pay his gambling losses and the construction costs on his new house. It's not inconceivable that this might lead a spoiled kid like Johnny Belmont to embezzlement. Then realizing that his embezzlement must eventually be discovered, the next logical step might well be murder.

Of one's own brother? Like most PIs, McGuffin was a romantic, knew it and was usually careful to guard against it. Sometimes too careful. No matter how the evidence stacked up against Victor's little brother, McGuffin had a gut feeling that he was not a killer. He was probably fierce on the racetrack or polo field, but these were just games played by big kids. And that's all Johnny was, just a kid.

But then so too was Billy.

Searching for a better metaphor, he considered the bookmaker. Although usually unopposed to mayhem as a collection device, few are so shortsighted as to resort to homicide. If Johnny's book was behind the bomb, it was unlikely that it was meant for his debtor's car. Was it possible then that the disgruntled bookie ordered Johnny's big brother to be blown up in the hope that it might induce him to hurry his payment?

It was possible. But extreme.

The murky overture evoking goblins and witches and mysterious beasts of the sinister forest gave way suddenly to the whirring suggestion of beating wings as McGuffin glided the car through a banked turn and thought of Conrad Daniels—family man, bag man, lawyer, socialite and mobster. If he and Johnny were closer than they claimed, so close that Daniels was aware of Johnny's financial problems, was it possible that he would do a favor for his friend and kill his brother?

It was entirely possible. For even though Daniels might be saddened by the loss of the goose that laid his golden eggs, his grief would be significantly lessened at becoming Johnny's partner in the Belmont Organization. And once

Johnny's partner, how long before he became the sole proprietor? Although this scenario too had possibilities, it was marred by the fact that it was Daniels who had tipped him off to Johnny's embezzlement. What if anything could Daniels gain by blowing the whistle on his intended partner? The case was still rife with unanswered questions, not the least of which was, Did Victor authorize Johnny to pay for his house with company funds, or didn't he?

"He said what?" Victor Belmont shouted over the phone.

"That you told him to charge his house to the company," McGuffin enunciated clearly into the receiver for the second time.

"Where the hell would he get an idea like that?"

"Then he's lying?" McGuffin asked gently.

"I didn't say that," Victor responded. "Listen, this has me confused, I don't want it to go any further for the time being. Not until I've had a chance to investigate and talk to Johnny. Do you understand?"

"Perfectly," McGuffin answered. "What I don't understand is the corporate reorganization."

"Johnny cried on your shoulder about that, did he?" Victor asked in a weary voice. "That was for his own good. And the company's," he added. "Between Johnny's gambling and his crazy business schemes, he was threatening to destroy the company. I had to do something and a corporate reorganization accomplished both—put Johnny on a tight budget and took away his voice in the management of the company. Let's go over this some other time, okay, Amos? Right now I just want to have a drink and go to bed."

"I can understand that," McGuffin said.

He hung up the phone, walked across the room and plopped down on his own bed. Half a loaf was better than none.

Chapter 11

Two days went by and the meeting between the Belmont brothers still hadn't taken place. Johnny had returned to the city, but had failed to return his brother's calls, a bad sign, McGuffin suggested. But Victor insisted there was nothing sinister about it, Johnny was simply unreliable.

So why should I be surprised that he hasn't set up the meeting with his mistress as he said he would? Promise him anything, just get him out of here. Johnny Belmont didn't like confrontations, neither with his brother nor with his brother's investigator. The question is, what's he trying to avoid, a charge of embezzlement, or felony murder? For if Angelo Tieri had blown himself up while carrying out Johnny's orders, he would be charged with Tieri's murder.

If I can prove it, McGuffin added to himself, as he walked across the room and switched the television on. It was time for the local news at eleven, murder, rape, robbery and mayhem, followed by the review of a new musical comedy from London, apparently because there was nothing to laugh or sing about in New York. According to the reviewer, however, this week's offering was only a little less grim than the local news.

He was about to turn it off when it was announced that they were switching live to Brooklyn where the body of Nina Tieri had just been found in the basement of the funeral parlor below her apartment. He stood motionless before the screen while a young man with blond curls pointed out the rent-controlled apartment where Nina Tieri had lived until a short while ago, and the Scalessi Funeral Home below, where her knifed body was found in the undertaker's basement workroom. A group of local youths stood behind the announcer, enjoying their moment of celebrity, while he described Nina Tieri's place in history, secured by marriage to the man who was killed while trying to plant a bomb on Victor Belmont's car.

When the announcer concluded with "Now back to the studio," McGuffin grabbed his jacket and bolted for the door.

The morgue truck was still parked in front of the Scalessi Funeral Home when McGuffin's cab pulled up, along with a few blue-and-whites parked at careless angles, roof lamps spinning. McGuffin got as far as the entrance to the funeral parlor when a big cop stepped in front of him.

"Where do you think you're going?"

"I'm a private investigator working for Victor Belmont," McGuffin explained, waving his California license quickly under the cop's nose. "Who's in charge of the investigation?"

"Lieutenant Dantley—so far," the cop answered. "Wait here, I'll see if he wants to talk to you."

McGuffin waited while the cop stepped inside and disappeared behind a red velvet curtain. He had witnessed enough violent death not to be squeamish about it, but just the thought of what undertakers did to corpses was more than enough to make him queasy. He hoped Lieutenant Dantley would come outside to talk to him.

"Follow me," the cop said, pulling the velvet curtain back.

"Shit—" McGuffin mumbled, as he followed the cop through the anteroom and the chapel where an old man lay in an open casket. Beyond another set of dark draperies, they passed through a side door into the first-floor hallway leading to Nina Tieri's apartment, then down the back stairs to the undertaker's workroom.

On a steel table with troughs leading to a floor drain lay

the body of a young man covered only by a coil of rubber hose. Oblivious to this, a group of cops and coroner's people were huddled over the body of Nina Tieri. She was wearing the same slacks she was wearing when McGuffin last saw her, but he couldn't be sure about the blouse. It was soaked almost completely with blood. While McGuffin was staring at the horribly sliced body, he became aware of someone speaking to him, a slightly built man in a cheap dark suit, the kind favored by plainclothesmen not for anonymity, but because they know it'll soon be ripped or stained.

"Yeah, I'm Belmont's private—McGuffin, Amos," he answered.

"Whattaya got for me, Amos?" the homicide inspector asked. "You know a butcher?"

"I got a few ideas," McGuffin answered.

"Let's hear 'em."

"If you tell me how it happened it might sharpen my suspicions," McGuffin countered. If he had nothing to trade, the homicide detective would give him nothing. It was the same on both coasts and all points in between.

"You ain't jerkin' my chain, are you?" Dantley asked.

"I think that my stirring things up could have had something to do with this. So tell me what happened and I'll tell you who I stirred up," McGuffin proposed.

Dantley considered for a moment, then nodded. "The way we got it from the sister-in-law, she had just come back from leavin' off the baby around ten o'clock. She musta started up to her apartment—we found her purse on the stairs with the money still in it—when she seen somebody on the landing. Then she turned around and ran back downstairs to the basement door at the end of the hall, then down the stairs to here," he said, pointing to the body. "That's as far as she got before the guy got to her. There was nothin' sexual, but the way he cut her up, it looks like he was enjoyin' himself."

"So how do you figure it?" McGuffin asked.

Dantley shrugged. "Homicide in the commission of a robbery. You got anything else?"

"Why'd the killer leave the purse?"

"He didn't see it," the cop answered, untroubled.

"Why did she run down here?" McGuffin asked, gesturing about him, to the corpse and the clinical tools of the undertaker's trade.

"Because she knew the door is always open—so the tenants can get to the boiler."

"So she ran into a dead end, a morbid place like this, rather than out the front door and into the street? Why would she do that?"

"She was confused."

"Uh-uh," McGuffin said. "She didn't go out the front door because there was somebody blocking her way. This was a professional hit, a man up and a man down. They didn't know about the open door at the end of the hall so it got a little sloppy, but it was professional all the same."

"Okay, it was professional," Dantley agreed easily. "Now tell me something I don't know, like who ordered it."

"The same guy who ordered Victor Belmont's execution," McGuffin replied. "She told me she didn't know who her husband was working for, but apparently she was lying. Either that or somebody thought she knew something."

"Who? Who you been agitatin'?" Dantley asked.

"Conrad Daniels, Laird Strauss and Johnny Belmont. You know them?"

"I know who they are. And if I was to make an educated guess, I'd say Conrad Daniels, just because of the company he keeps."

"Then go get him, with my blessing," McGuffin said.

A faint smile crossed Lieutenant Dantley's face as he considered this. The cop who could put Conrad Daniels away might make police commissioner, or even mayor! Suddenly the smile disappeared as it probably occurred to him, McGuffin guessed, that it was also an easy way to make it to an early grave.

Chapter 12

The Dona Bella, the last sports bar on Strauss's list, was a supper club in the east Fifties with a canopy and a large pair of potted ferns flanking a carved door. Beside the door was a picture of a sloe-eyed chanteuse caressing a microphone while coming out of her dress. A uniformed doorman opened the door with a salute and McGuffin was passed into the bookie's lair.

He checked his coat in the narrow foyer, then stepped into the darkly carpeted bar, dimly lighted by gold cherubs on mahogany-paneled walls holding electric candles suggesting giant phalluses. Directly opposite the red-lacquered bar was a fountain featuring a nude woman pouring water from a pitcher, surrounded by a picket fence of red and blue dancing waters. There were several patrons clustered around the end of the bar and a couple of waitresses setting tables in the dining room, but other than that the place was empty.

McGuffin took a stool near the center of the bar, a respectful distance from the gold-chain, tie-crossed-over-the-paunch types huddled at the end, and stared at the pictures of Italian fighters taped to the mirror while he waited for the bartender to break away. He was in no hurry, grinning as he was at a tale being told by someone in the middle of the huddle. After the punchline and a burst of laughter, the young bartender moved languidly down the bar, eyelids drooping sullenly, weighed down perhaps by scar tissue.

"Whull i' be?"

"Club soda."

"Club soda?"

"With a Black Label back." He would pay for it but not enjoy it.

He nodded and went for the high shelf while McGuffin returned to the pictures on the mirror. He found the one he was looking for, the bartender, a few years before, slamming a left into the ribs of a black fighter as he was falling to the canvas—the great white fantasy. The blank space next to it, followed by a couple of baseball pictures, was where the photo of the black fighter knocking the bartender through the ropes a few minutes later had once stood, McGuffin guessed. When the bartender placed his drinks in front of him, McGuffin pointed at the picture and asked, "That you?"

"Yeah, dat's me. The night I retired." McGuffin smiled. He was right. "I useta be a fightah on'y now I'm an actuh. You ain't in the business by any chance?"

"Sorry," McGuffin said, shaking his head. "But I have a close friend at the Actors Company."

"No shit. Who you know there?"

"Franz Tutin."

"Oh wow, Franz Tutin!" the bartender exclaimed, his formerly sullen eyes beginning to dance. "The man's a fuckin' legend."

"He'd agree," McGuffin said.

"My name's Danny Biando, useta be Danny the Destroyer," he said, sticking a hand across the bar.

McGuffin introduced himself and shook the Destroyer's hand, which felt more like a light cruiser. Danny Biando was well advised to become an actor.

"Listen, Amos," he began, leaning confidentially across the bar, "I know you never seen my work or nuttin', but I'm doin' a scene next week in my actin' class and if you like to come it'll be an honor. And if you could get me an audition wit' Franz Tutin, man, wow, I'd really appreciate it."

"I'll see what I can do," McGuffin promised.

"Wow, tha'd be great, man."

"What play are you doing?"

"*Cyrano de Bergerac*. It's French."

McGuffin nodded. "And you play the tongue-tied soldier."

The actor was stung. "Fuck, man, I play Cyrano."

"Of course." So Franz Tutin wasn't the only larcenous acting teacher in New York. "Tell me," McGuffin said, leaning in and speaking softly, "do you know where I can find Gregory Scott?"

"Right there," he said, jerking a thumb at the knot of drinkers at the end of the bar.

"Would you tell him that Mr. Belmont's agent would like a word with him?" McGuffin said, sliding a ten-dollar bill across the bar.

If he could move his hands that fast in the ring he'd be a champ today, McGuffin thought, as he watched the ten disappear. A few moments later the society bookie approached.

"Johnny Belmont sent you?" he asked, looking McGuffin up and down.

"I represent the family," McGuffin qualified, before introducing himself.

Gregory Scott was young, not much over thirty, thin and bespectacled, with light-brown hair parted in the middle. He wore a madras shirt under a frayed crew neck sweater under a gray tweed jacket. The society bookmaker had not just attended an Ivy League school, he had never gotten over it.

"You're not what I expected," McGuffin said.

"Neither is Johnny." Although there was an amused smile on his thin lips, McGuffin suspected it was camouflage, like his preppy clothes.

"How much does he owe?"

"You're his agent, you tell me."

"A hundred thousand?"

"More than that. And I get the feeling Johnny didn't send you here to give it to me."

"No, I don't have your money, that's not why I'm here."

"Then why are you here?"

"To ask you some questions about Angelo Tieri."

"Never heard of him."

"Come on, Gregory, you read the sports pages. The

86

utility infielder who played for a while with the Cubs, the Brooklyn bomber.''

"The Brooklyn bomber, that's very funny," Scott said. "Yeah, I know who you mean, but I never met the guy. Why do you ask?"

McGuffin shrugged. "I just thought you might know him, seeing as how he almost did you a big favor."

"I don't get you."

"I don't suppose it ever occurred to you, but if Johnny should have inherited his brother's half of the company, you'd be reasonably assured of getting your money, wouldn't you?"

"You're right, that never occurred to me," the book-maker answered, still smiling.

"Some people suspect that the bomb was meant for Johnny's car, but you and I both know better than that, don't we?"

"Do we?"

"Or at least we hope it wasn't. After all, it's rather difficult to collect a gambling debt from the estate of a deceased, isn't it?"

"Impossible."

"Exactly. So if you thought anybody was trying to harm your client, you'd be a little worried."

"I'd be very worried."

"But you're not," McGuffin pointed out.

"Are you saying I should be? That the bomb was meant for Johnny, not Victor?"

"I'm quite sure of it," McGuffin said. "In the dark, to a man who had never been there before, Victor's Mercedes could have easily been mistaken for Johnny's."

"Bullshit," the society bookmaker interjected. "Even a guy who can't see a curve ball can tell the difference between a sedan and a two-hundred-thousand-dollar limousine."

"Who said it was a limousine?" McGuffin asked.

"It was in the papers, for Christ's sake! What the hell are you, some kind of cop?"

"Some kind," McGuffin answered. "I'm a private detective working for Victor Belmont."

87

"I'd like to help, but I don't know anything about it."

"You have any idea who Angelo Tieri might have been working for?"

Gregory Scott pursed his lips thoughtfully before replying "I'd look to the competition."

"Good idea," McGuffin said.

"If you'll excuse me, I have to get back to my friends," he said, sliding off the barstool.

"Thanks for your help," McGuffin said.

"Anytime," Scott called.

Outside the uniformed doorman whistled up a cab and McGuffin instructed the driver to take him back to his hotel. It was possible that a man whose business was sports could have forgotten that the bomber was a professional athlete yet remember that the blown car was a limousine, he thought as he raced south on Park Avenue. Not likely, but possible.

However, it wasn't at all likely that the bookmaker should react so calmly when told that one of his principal debtors was about to shuffle off this mortal coil. Not unless he was certain that the information was wrong and that Victor Belmont, not his little brother, was the intended victim. And he could only be certain of this if he had been informed by someone reliable or if it was he who had sent Angelo to place the bomb on Victor's limousine.

The first theory had merit, but McGuffin preferred the second. It explained why Scott would have at first denied knowing that Angelo Tieri was the bomber—the kneejerk reaction of the co-conspirator—while at the same time explaining why Scott was able to identify Victor's automobile. It wasn't because he had read of it in the papers, it was because he had carefully rehearsed Angelo Tieri before sending him off to plant a bomb on Victor Belmont's limousine.

Or at least it was a possibility.

"What about motive?" Victor Belmont asked, when McGuffin conveyed these thoughts the following morning.

88

They were in the architectural offices of Greene, Smith and Krust, high above midtown Third Avenue, studying the proposed model for Victor's Hudson River landfill project, Belmont City. The project was dominated by two high towers at either end of the table, with a hodgepodge of smaller buildings between, some resembling pyramids, others observatories. Three piers surrounded by yachts and adorned with more futuristic buildings jutted out into the Hudson River where the Belmont Fountain was spewing water into the air. The fountain would add oxygen to the water so that the bass could breathe easier, Victor had explained with a conspiratorial grin.

"His motive was to frighten Johnny into paying off his debt," the detective answered, as he slowly followed his client around the Ping Pong–size table.

"Killing me over Johnny's debt seems a bit extreme, even for a mobster like Gregory Scott," Victor said.

"Scott didn't intend to kill you. He assumed the chauffeur always started the car in the garage by himself before driving around to the front of the house to pick you up. Scott's an ice man, he has no compunction about killing a chauffeur if it'll scare Johnny into paying up."

"But why would Scott assume that I never get into the car with my chauffeur? Or that I don't sometimes drive myself?"

"Because Johnny told him you don't."

"Johnny—?" he asked, snapping his head around.

"Relax, it was entirely innocent. Scott could have picked Johnny's brain without Johnny ever knowing what was happening."

"But Johnny knows that I always walk to the garage with the chauffeur and we get into the car together."

McGuffin's chin dropped. "Always?"

"It's a ritual," Victor answered.

"You're absolutely sure Johnny is aware of this?" McGuffin questioned.

"Of course I'm sure," Victor answered. "Johnny used to make fun of me because of it. If his bookmaker asked, Johnny would have had to tell him that I'm always in the car when the chauffeur starts the engine."

"Okay, let's not jump to any conclusions," McGuffin said. "I only assumed that Scott got his information from Johnny, but now it's obvious that he didn't."

"Is it?" Victor asked.

"I don't understand," McGuffin said. "Johnny obviously embezzled money from the company, he refuses to explain why, he won't return your calls or mine, and yet until now you've insisted he's just an irresponsible kid. Now suddenly you think he and his bookmaker conspired to kill you?"

"I know I must sound confused and believe me, I don't like it any more than you do. It's this second murder, this Nina Tieri thing that bothers me. I can't help thinking that if I hadn't put you on the case she might not have been killed."

"And if cows had wings they might be able to fly," McGuffin replied. "Nina Tieri was killed because she knew who hired her husband to kill you. You and I might have moved it along, but it had to happen sooner or later. Guys like Gregory Scott are very uncomfortable with living witnesses. Daniels too, and probably Strauss as well. The question now is Johnny."

"I know," Victor said, looking down at the model of Belmont City. "I told you that Johnny would never do anything to harm me and that's true. I'd like to think it's because he loves me as much as I love him, but there's another reason. Johnny doesn't have what it takes. He's a spoiled, lazy, selfish kid, for which I'm at least partly to blame. I tried to get him to take an active role in the business, but it was a disaster. He put us in the theater business, the movie business and finally a big ski resort that went belly up. Between his business schemes and his gambling, he cost me millions. And when I had to take away his vote and cut back on his allowance, he sulked like a baby.

"Don't misunderstand," he said, looking up at McGuffin. "I still don't believe that Johnny would ever try to kill me. But I'm no longer so sure that he would do everything he could to stop someone else from doing it," he added in a weak voice.

90

McGuffin said nothing for a long time. The pain in Victor Belmont's face precluded any false assurances. The realization that his little brother might be moved by greed if not to murder him, then to allow somebody else to do it was an idea he had fought until he no longer had the strength to resist. It was a conclusion McGuffin had at first subtly urged upon his client and ardently wished. To write off the man who stood to gain the most by Victor Belmont's death, brother or no, flew squarely in the face of all logic. Yet now, with his success, McGuffin was suddenly uncertain.

"It's entirely possible that we're both stepping off on the wrong foot," McGuffin said. "Scott could have ordered that bomb placed on your car without a care for who it might kill, you or your chauffeur or both of you. If it was you, Johnny would have the money to pay him; if it was the chauffeur, he'd damn sure find it."

Belmont smiled weakly and thanked the detective. "I appreciate all you've done," he assured him.

"I haven't done anything yet," McGuffin answered. "I can't prove that Gregory Scott was behind it until I can somehow connect him to the bomber. And I sure as hell can't say that your brother had anything to do with it."

"Nor would I like you to."

"What do you mean?"

"I'll give Johnny the money to pay off his bookie. And I'll give Johnny the benefit of the doubt," he added. "But just to be sure, I'll also change my will."

"But what if we're wrong? What if it's somebody else who's trying to kill you?"

"Such as?"

"Conrad Daniels. I know, you're the goose that lays the golden eggs. But that wouldn't change if Johnny took over. In fact, it would even get better. Johnny's no match for Daniels, he'd soon have the whole company."

"When my lawyers get through tightening up my will, I'll make it quite clear to Conrad that he has nothing to gain by my death."

"What about Laird Strauss? He could kill you just because of this," McGuffin said, pointing to the model of

91

Belmont City. "Or it could be somebody we haven't even considered. If you leave this thing unresolved, you might very well be killing yourself."

Victor Belmont smiled somewhat patronizingly. "I appreciate your dedication, Amos, I really do. And I want you to know there's a generous golden parachute in this for you."

"Golden parachute—? This isn't about my fee, this is about your life. I don't care what you pay me or don't pay me, I don't like unfinished cases. But even more than that, I don't like dead clients. So you can do what you like with that golden parachute, but I'm not quitting until I find the guy who's trying to blow you away."

Victor Belmont stared incredulously at the detective. "I'm amazed. In all my years in business, you're the first man I've ever met who was eager to work for nothing."

"I wouldn't say eager," McGuffin qualified. "But if it was to be that way, I'll work for nothing."

"I believe you," Belmont said, reaching for McGuffin's hand. "Congratulations, you've got the job. At your old salary," he added.

On the way out the door they passed a second model. In contrast to the pink spires, golden domes and glass roofs of Belmont City, this looked like a mud hut washed up onto the river shore.

"What the hell is that?" McGuffin asked.

"That's the alternate model for Belmont City. It's the ugliest building my architect could come up with, but it conforms exactly to the building code. If I should decide to build that monstrosity, there's very little the city could do to stop me. But being a civic-spirited gentleman, I'll give the city fathers their choice. Shall I build this beautiful model, whose glorious spires stretch somewhat beyond the height the law allows, or shall I build this shit-brown but legal warehouse? The choice, ladies and gentlemen, is yours."

Actually, McGuffin thought, as he followed the developer into the next room, the tall spires with their jumble of outbuildings weren't that much an improvement over the mud hut. In the next room they passed a long row of cubicles containing architects bent over their drawing boards, some presumably working on beautiful large buildings, others ugly small ones. The one to be built would be decided later in a game of chicken between the developer and the planning board. Belmont walked McGuffin as far as the elevator where he wished him luck and shook hands a second time.

"By the way, what can you tell me about Antonia Ruiz?" McGuffin asked.

"Who?"

"Johnny's mistress, the woman he says was with him the night of the explosion."

Victor looked at him with a perplexed expression and shook his head. "There was nobody with Johnny that night."

"You're sure?" McGuffin asked, as the elevator door slid open.

"I'm positive. His car lights woke me up when he arrived. I walked to the window and I watched him get out of the car by himself and go into his house alone."

"Thanks," McGuffin said, then the door closed and the elevator began its rapid descent.

Chapter 13

Over the next two days McGuffin made several attempts to contact Johnny Belmont without any success. He finally phoned his wife at the television studio where she was taping her show, *Penny's From Manhattan*. She was about to interview a plastic surgeon but she took the time to tell McGuffin that she had no idea where her husband was, then returned to the set. Ironically McGuffin was watching a previously taped segment of the *Penny's From Manhattan* show in his hotel room while speaking to her. She had terrific legs, which she kept crossing and uncrossing while eagerly interviewing a thin man with silver hair and a deep tan, who had founded something called the Glowing Self. No mere spa, it was a kind of chain of overhaul shops where one could be manicured, pedicured, exercised, trimmed, toned, tanned, massaged, shampooed, cut, dyed and styled and taught how to speak without a regional accent. The fact that the founder of Glowing Self spoke with a lisp did not cause Penny to question this last service.

When Penny's long legs were interrupted by a commercial, McGuffin switched the television off and dialed Marilyn's apartment.

"I'm not speaking to you," she informed him.

"Come on, Marilyn—" he pleaded.

"Is this conversation being recorded?"

"Of course not. What do you think I am?"

"You're a prick, that's what you are! Do you realize that

94

shyster lawyer of yours had some sleazy PI asking personal questions about me at the Actors Company? He even asked Mr. Tutin what drugs I use, who my lesbian lover is and who my orgy partners are!"

"I didn't authorize that."

"How considerate. But that doesn't change the fact that my career is being damaged, and it's also taking a toll on Hillary."

"Believe me, Marilyn, I don't want this any more than you do. That's why I called—I want to take you and Hillary out to dinner. I want to discuss this in a calm rational manner."

"I can't."

"What do you mean you can't? Why not?"

"My lawyer told me not to speak to you."

"Your lawyer? You have a lawyer?"

"That's right, I have a lawyer," she answered. "Do you think you can have one but I can't?"

"No, of course not."

"And if you're wondering where I got the money, my women's support group is paying for it," she informed him in a gloating tone. "Hilda may not be as high priced as your shyster lawyer, but she's dedicated. And mean. She says that when she gets done with you, your daughter will be nothing to you but a face on a milk carton."

"Marilyn, this is getting out of hand," McGuffin said.

"You started it."

"You're the one who took Hillary out of the state."

"Which Hilda says I have every right to do."

"Marilyn—"

"I can't talk to you any more. If you have anything to say, have your lawyer call Hilda. Good-bye," she said and hung up.

"Hilda—" McGuffin said numbly, as he replaced the receiver. He imagined her as the fat commandant of a concentration camp where he and hundreds of other divorced fathers watched from behind barbed wire while their oblivious children and their mothers cavorted freely in the verdant fields beyond.

Johnny Belmont phoned the next morning. He was well launched on his excited tirade before McGuffin was fully awake.

"You lied to me!" he charged, stopping Johnny in midsentence.

"What do you mean?"

"You said you were with your girlfriend on the night of the explosion, but your brother told me you were alone in the house that night."

"That's not true," Johnny insisted.

"Why would he lie about something like that?"

"He didn't. Victor didn't know she was in the house with me because I didn't want him to know. He and his wife get on my case about other women, so I had to sneak her in. She hid in the house until after they took me to the hospital, then she split."

"Victor watched from his bedroom window when you arrived. He said you were the only one who got out of the car and walked into the house," McGuffin informed him.

"I was the only one he saw," Johnny corrected. "Don't you think I know he watches when I drive up? I had her wait in the car for five minutes, then follow me in. We do it all the time, she'll tell you."

"When?"

"That's what I'm trying to tell you, she's disappeared."

"Johnny, I'm from San Francisco, not Peoria," McGuffin said with exaggerated patience.

"I'm telling you the truth!" he wailed. "She didn't show up for work, she's not at her apartment and her doorman hasn't seen her for two days! I'm afraid something might have happened to her."

"And I'm afraid something's happening to me. I'm afraid somebody's leading me up the garden path, only I'm not going any farther. The only path I'm taking with you is the one that leads to the district attorney's office."

"If you don't believe me, go to the club where she works. They'll tell you exactly what I'm telling you."

"What club?"

"The Dona Bella."

"Dona Bella?"

"Yeah, she's their singer."

"The one with the big—"

"Yeah, Tanya, one name, short for Antonia."

Dona Bella—Belladonna. It was suddenly so obvious. The Poison Club, as it was known to Nina Tieri and other mob wives, was the club where Angelo Tieri hung out with Conrad Daniels. The club Daniels denied knowing anything about.

"Tell me, Johnny, how did you meet Tanya?"

"How? I don't know, somebody at the club introduced me."

"Your bookmaker, Gregory Scott?"

"It could have been him," he replied uncertainly.

"Or Conrad Daniels? Did you ever see him at the Dona Bella?"

"Yeah, several times."

"Did he introduce you to Tanya?"

Johnny thought about this for a moment, then confessed that he couldn't remember. "There was a whole bunch of us in the bar and she just sort of appeared. I was a little drunk, if you know what I mean."

McGuffin knew what he meant. "During the time you were with her, did Tanya ever exhibit any unusual interest in Victor, his schedule, his routine—his car?"

Johnny's laugh came softly over the wire. "I don't think Tanya ever exhibited any interest in anything beside fucking. She was the best, the fucking best."

"Why do you say was?"

"I don't know," he said after a moment. "It just came out that way. Will you see if you can find her, Amos? I'll pay."

"I'll see what I can do," McGuffin answered. It occurred to him that Johnny might pay dearly.

*　　*　　*

97

Conrad Daniels's law office on East Fifty-ninth Street had the look and feel of a designer's room. Three walls of his plushly carpeted and padded office were neatly lined with gleaming leather volumes, none of them exhibiting so much as a sprained, let alone broken, spine, and his burled walnut desk was as clean as any in the Pentagon. There were several photographs flanking the window behind the lawyer's desk, one of them a group of hunters at the foot of a mountain.

"You've got a very neat office," McGuffin said, as he took a seat opposite the desk.

"I leave the nuts and bolts of the law to others," Daniels replied.

McGuffin pointed to the photograph on the wall. "I see you're a hunter."

Daniels looked over his shoulder, then back at the detective. "Just a group of friends."

"Taken at your hunting lodge?"

"Not *my* hunting lodge," Daniels answered.

"I thought you owned one."

"You must be thinking of somebody else."

"Maybe," McGuffin said.

The lawyer glanced at his Rolex. "You said you have something important to ask me."

"Yes, I do. It's about the Poison Club."

"It seems to me you asked me about that once before and I told you, I've never heard of it."

"But you have heard of the Dona Bella Club."

The lawyer missed a beat before replying, "I'm familiar with it."

"Do you own it?"

Daniels smiled and shook his head. "Hardly. It just happens to be a sports joint where a lot of my friends hang out."

"Gregory Scott, the society bookie?"

"Among others."

"Angelo Tieri?"

"I might have seen him there."

"What about Tanya?"

"So, you've met Tanya," he said, his dark eyes widening with the pleasure McGuffin must have felt.

"No, I haven't. And I'm worried that I might never get the chance." Daniels said he didn't understand, so McGuffin explained her disappearance.

"Missing?" he repeated, a new concept to the mob lawyer. "Why would she want to do a thing like that?"

"Maybe it was somebody else's idea."

"Whose?"

"The guy who sent Angelo to blow up Victor."

Conrad Daniels's soft eyes fastened hard on McGuffin's. "And do you know who that might be?"

"No, but Tanya certainly does. Or did," McGuffin corrected. "And whoever that person is, he heard that I wanted to talk to Tanya and he became worried. Now that Nina Tieri's dead, Tanya's the only remaining witness who can connect him with Angelo, so he killed her."

Daniels looked up from his fingernails and said, "Then we might never know who tried to kill Victor."

"I like to think that when a man commits three crimes rather than one, my chances of catching him are three times as good as before."

"Are they?"

"I'm sure of it. I was confused for a while—unfamiliar territory, you know—but right now I feel I'm very close to solving this case."

"Let's hope so," Daniels said. "For Victor's sake."

The lawyer rolled his wrist over, the signal that the interview was over. "Was there anything else you wanted to ask me?"

"Not for now."

"Then let me wish you good hunting," Daniels said, climbing to his feet.

"I can find my way out," McGuffin said, pulling himself out of the chair.

"One other thing," Daniels said, as McGuffin walked to

the door. McGuffin stopped and turned. "You asked me to find out if Angelo had worked on Johnny Belmont's house."

"Yeah?"

"He didn't."

"Thanks," McGuffin said, then opened the door and left.

The poster of the voluptuous Tanya had been removed, McGuffin noted, as he stepped out of the cab and hurried into the Dona Bella Club. It was the middle of the afternoon, the lull between lunch and the cocktail hour, and the place was nearly empty, which McGuffin had counted on. He had some questions for the bartender that he didn't want shared with the society bookie or any of the crossed-tie set.

He found Danny crouched behind the bar, humming along with Barbra Streisand while stacking Heinekens in the cooler. When McGuffin greeted him he looked up, more heavily lidded than usual, nodded mutely and went back to his bottles. McGuffin waited until he had finished, then ordered a club soda with a Black Label back.

"I see you've taken down Tanya's poster," McGuffin observed. "What happened, she get another job?"

Danny rolled his thick shoulders, presumably a gesture of ignorance. He took his time with the drinks, then informed McGuffin, "Ten dollahs."

"The prices have gone up considerably." Danny nodded with his eyelids. "Conrad Daniels does still own the place, doesn't he?" McGuffin asked.

"I wouldn't know," Danny said. He picked the twenty up and turned to the cash register.

"The Poison Club, that's what Angelo Tieri used to call it." Danny rang up McGuffin's drink, then turned and slapped McGuffin's ten on the bar. "As a matter of fact, that blank space on the mirror—between you and the ballplayers—that's where Angelo's picture used to hang, isn't it?"

Danny turned to the mirror, then back to McGuffin. "Is it?"

When McGuffin pushed the ten across the car, Danny pushed it back. McGuffin pretended not to notice. He could

100

not fail to notice, however, that Conrad Daniels had gotten to Danny ahead of him, probably within minutes of his office visit. But Danny Biando had one weakness of which the lawyer was probably only dimly aware; while McGuffin, having lived and suffered with an actress, understood all too well just how far an actor might go to satisfy this cursed ambition.

"I've been talking to Franz Tutin about you," McGuffin said. Danny's hooded eyes betrayed nothing. "I told him you reminded me of the young Brando and he got very excited." The lids fluttered faintly. "So much so that I might even be able to get him to come and watch your performance tomorrow night."

McGuffin watched while fear and loyalty wrestled with naked ambition. "Who you think you're shittin'? You don't know no Franz Tutin," Danny replied in a firm voice that nevertheless betrayed a desperate wish to be wrong.

McGuffin shrugged. "If that's the way you feel—"

He picked up his ten and slid off the stool without having touched either of his drinks. He got as far as the fountain when Danny called, "Hey, McGuffin!"

"Yeah?"

"Can I trust you to keep your mouth shut?"

McGuffin took a card from his pocket and held it up. "Confidential investigations," he said. "With me it's a sacred trust."

"It better be," the bartender said. " 'Cuz when I go against certain people, I'm givin' 'way a lotta weight, if you know what I mean."

"I know what you mean."

"You bring Tutin and we'll talk."

"I'll bring him," McGuffin promised, then turned and walked out of the Poison Club.

"You vut?" Franz Tutin exclaimed.

"As a favor to Mr. Belmont," McGuffin said.

"I vuld not go across the street to vatch the Old Vic do

101

Cyrano de Bergerac, but you vant me to vatch a student production? You're even crazier than your vife says."

"I know, it's a strange request," McGuffin agreed. "That's what I should have told Mr. Belmont, but he's the guy who's paying my salary, so what could I do? Mr. Belmont thinks the kid might have talent, but he wants your professional opinion. You know how it is, Mr. Tutin."

"Yes, I know very vell how it is," he said, grasping the lion head arms of his massive desk chair and thrusting his chunky body into the air. "They call it charity ven in fact it is slavery. In return for a few hundred thousand dollars I must always be on call, to go to their parties and meet their stupid friends, weekends in the Hamptons, winter in the Caribbean— I am no longer sure—am I the artist or am I the whore?"

"The artist," McGuffin said. "Definitely. And like any great artist, you're willing to sacrifice for your art."

Franz Tutin paced his office, weighing his future, while all the famous alums of the Actors Company waited on the wall for his decision. "This is very important to Victor, is it?"

"It's a matter of life and death," McGuffin replied.

"Art requires great sacrifices of us all, but this is truly absurd," the great director said finally. "Very vell, I'll do it."

McGuffin thanked him profusely, then fairly ran to the phone in the lobby. Danny was excited but his instincts prevailed.

"If you're bullshittin' me, McGuffin, I'm gonna bust your face," he warned.

"Now why would I want to bullshit you?" McGuffin asked.

"Because you want somethin'," he answered.

"Danny, I'm doing this for you because I love the theater. If, however, you should choose to reward me with the answers to a few harmless questions, I'll be most grateful."

"Harmless." He snorted. "You don't know from fuckin' harmless."

"Danny, I'm the soul of discretion. Franz and I will see you tonight at eight. Break a leg."

"Don't say dat."

The Institute of Theatrical Arts on the Upper East Side of
Manhattan claimed almost as many distinguished graduates
as the Actors Company, which was why—until this historic
evening, initiated by a San Francisco civilian—Franz Tutin
had never set foot in the place. Word that he was in the
audience set the place abuzz with a drama and comedy that
the classic *Cyrano de Bergerac* would be hard-pressed to
follow. Only Danny Biando, applying his putty nose before
a cracked mirror, was calm in the face of such distinguished
attention. Stage fright was nothing compared to the trouble
he might find himself in after he answered McGuffin's
questions.

Danny Biando's scene was second on the program. The
audience applauded politely at the conclusion of the first
scene while Franz groaned softly. Then the director returned to center stage to announce the next exercise, the
balcony scene from *Cyrano de Bergerac*.

The curtain parts to reveal a balcony lighted by moon-
light, and Christian, a despondent young Guardsman, seated
on a garden bench. Danny Biando, wearing a nose resembling a blue cucumber, lunges suddenly from the wings,
cape atwirl, spies his comrade in arms and demands, "Wha's
a mattuh?"

"Oi vey—" Franz muttered.

Christian leaps to his feet and in a high breathless voice
informs Cyrano that his love for the fair Roxanne will be
doomed, unless Cyrano will substitute his own eloquent
voice for the hapless lover's. Cyrano agrees and as the
somewhat chunky Roxanne steps out onto the balcony, he
conceals himself and begins his ventriloquist's act. At Cyrano's first speech, "Troo da wahm summah gloom my woids
grope da dahkness for you," his peers began to titter.

Seizing his sword, Danny stepped downstage and out of
character, and glowered at his audience until the theater
was silent as death. Even Franz Tutin was speechless, whether
from shock or intimidation. Meanwhile the corpulent Rox-

anne, who was exerting a noticeable strain on the balcony, had recited her speech in a southern drawl, and it was back to Danny.

"My haht's open and waitin' for dem—too lahg a mahk to miss. My woids fly home, heavy wit' honey like retoinin' bees—"

"Give me strength," Franz pleaded softly, as he slid down in his seat where he remained for the remainder of Danny's performance.

When it was mercifully over, Franz rose and fled, followed by McGuffin.

"A young Brando!" he exclaimed. "The man is a young vegetable!"

"I know," McGuffin agreed, hurrying after him. He caught him at the corner and laid a hand on his arm. "But Mr. Belmont wants you to be kind to him."

"I'll be kind! Tell him I said to get a job in a gas station. That's the kindest advice I can give."

"No," McGuffin said. "You've got to go back and offer him encouragement."

"Encouragment! You are insane! To encourage that—that Neanderthal, vould be the cruelest thing I could do."

"I agree, but Mr. Belmont particularly asked that you go backstage and say something nice to the kid, even if he bombs."

"I don't understand," Franz said, shaking his head. "Why should Victor vant to encourage that boy?" Suddenly the answer came to him. "Victor and that boy are—?"

McGuffin said nothing.

"My God—Victor— Just vhen I thought I'd seen it all."

"Now will you come backstage with me?"

Franz nodded dully and allowed McGuffin to lead him back to the theater where Danny Biando waited.

"Amazed!" Danny exploded, pounding a fist on the bar. "You hoid him; Franz Tutin was amazed by my performance."

"I hoid," McGuffin said.

"And stunned! 'In all my years in the theater, I have

rarely been so stunned by a performance,' " Danny repeated, doing a fair imitation of Tutin's accent.

"Unfettered by the constraints of technique," McGuffin added.

"I didn't get that one," he said, turning a puzzled face to McGuffin.

"He meant you're an original," McGuffin explained.

Danny smiled and lifted his Heineken to his lips. They were seated at the bar of an Irish pub a few blocks away from the scene of Danny's triumph.

"Man, the look on the students' faces when me and Mr. Tutin come outta the dressin' room—I gotta hand it to ya, McGuffin, you delivered."

"It was your talent that won him over," McGuffin reminded him.

"Dat's true." Danny raised his bottle, then had a thought. "The only ting is, he didn't say nuttin about no audition."

"He asked me to take care of that," McGuffin said.

"You?"

"It wouldn't be ethical for him to steal the institute's most promising student right from under the nose of the director. You understand."

"Yeah, sure. Like how long I gotta wait?"

"That depends," McGuffin answered. "But don't worry, I'm on the case." Danny watched and waited while McGuffin sipped his club soda, then carefully replaced it over its wet ring. "Let's talk about Tanya."

Danny looked over both shoulders, then back at McGuffin. "What about her?"

"Do you know what happened to her or where she might be?"

"Not a clue. She didn't call, she didn't talk to nobody. One night she just didn't show and nobody knows why, it's a fuckin' mystery."

"Who hired her?"

"Mr. Daniels."

"So Conrad does own the Dona Bella."

Danny opened his mouth to deny it, then replied hesitantly, "Not exactly. I mean he's the front man, but he's got partners. And don't ask me who dey are, 'cuz I wouldn't tell ya if I knew."

"You want to be a star, don't you?" McGuffin cautioned.

"Yeah, but I can't enjoy it if I'm dead," he answered.

"How did Johnny meet Tanya?"

Danny shrugged. "He just showed up at the club one night and they started goin' out."

"Could his bookie have introduced them?"

"Gregory? Yeah, he could have."

"Conrad Daniels?"

"Yeah, him too," he said, nodding. "Even Angelo."

"Angelo! Johnny knew Angelo Tieri?"

Danny laughed. "I guess you could say dat, seein' as how he took Angelo's girlfriend away from him."

"Tanya was Angelo's girlfriend?"

"She was nuts about him, I could never figure it. One minute she's talkin' about marryin' the guy and the next thing I know she drops him for Johnny Belmont. I guess any chick's gonna go for the money, but I'm tellin' ya, I was surprised."

So was McGuffin. He had been looking for the would-be murderer among the movers and shakers of Manhattan, when in fact his quarry might be no more than a jilted lover, so inept that he set his bomb for the wrong man. Danny, however, remained skeptical.

"I don't know," he said, when McGuffin had made his theory known. "Angelo just didn't seem to get all that worked up about it when Tanya dumped him. In fact, him and Johnny acted just like nothin' had happened."

"He could have been hiding it," McGuffin suggested.

Danny shook his head. "Angelo wasn't the type to keep things inside. If he wanted Johnny, he woulda gone after him right there in the club. Sneakin' around plantin' bombs, dat wasn't Angelo's way."

"With one exception that we know of," McGuffin qualified.

"Dat was somethin' else. Somebody hired him to plant dat bomb on Victor Belmont's car."

"Who?"

"Hey, McGuffin, I'm on the t'reshold of stardom—you tink I wanna die now? I'll tell you what I know, you make de calls, okay?"

McGuffin nodded. "What about Johnny and Conrad Daniels? Did you often see the two of them together?"

"I don't know how often, but yeah, I see 'em together once in a while. Only not since the bomb," he added. "After Conrad took Angelo's picture down, it's like nobody wants to know nobody else, if you know what I mean."

McGuffin knew what he meant. For a man who knew Conrad Daniels slightly, and Angelo Tieri not at all, Johnny Belmont spent a lot of time with both.

"Tell me about Gregory Scott. Did he know Angelo?"

"Know him? He was his runner—pickups and payouts—nuttin' big."

"Was he an enforcer?"

Danny shook his head as he slid the empty bottle across the bar. "He's got Tony Pliers for dat. Big guy, wears his tie crossed over his gut—?"

"Pliers?" McGuffin repeated.

"That's how he collects," Danny explained, imitating a lobster.

"Did Scott ever use a bomber that you know of?"

Danny shook his head. "Scott says five minutes wit' Tony Pliers is as good as a certified check."

"Do you think Scott would turn the pliers loose on Johnny Belmont?"

Danny's laugh resembled a snort. "Not unless he owed him a dollar or more. He'd send Tony after his own mother if she stiffed him. Scott ain't human, he's got a calculator where his heart's supposed to be." He picked up his empty bottle and rapped the bar. "Hey, Paddy, another beer!"

The bartender scowled but went to the cooler. McGuffin topped off his club soda, took a sip and asked, "If Tanya wanted to hide out, do you know where she'd go?"

"You got me. She worked in Vegas before she come here, she don't know nobody."

"Where's Conrad's hunting lodge?"

"You tink he's hiding her out?"

"It might be wishful thinking."

"I don' know where it is."

McGuffin didn't push. He had no intention of going up there, but if Tanya didn't turn up soon, there could be little doubt that she had died because she knew too much. And if she knew too much about Gregory Scott, she might, through the offices of Tony Pliers, show up in an automobile trunk at JFK, or in the East River. But if it turned out that it was Conrad Daniels about whom she knew too much, McGuffin would suggest that the local cops comb the hunting lodge property for a fresh grave.

When he had all the information from Danny that he was going to get, he thanked him and paid for their drinks, leaving a generous tip to soothe the Irish bartender's abraded feelings. He offered to drop Danny at his apartment, but he preferred to go back to the theater. There was a cast party in progress, and although McGuffin counseled against it, Danny thought it would be a good time to announce his coming audition with the Actors Company.

There was a message when he got back to his hotel. Laird Strauss wanted to see him first thing in the morning.

call from a girl, a friend of hers, but she wouldn't identify herself. She said Tanya asked her to call and tell me that she wouldn't see me for a while because there was a private detective looking for her and she had to go away."

"Did she give you any idea where she was going?"

"None."

"Or why she couldn't talk to me?"

"The girl didn't seem to know exactly what it was all about herself, except that somebody wanted Tanya to talk to you, to tell you something that wasn't true. She didn't want to do it, but she was afraid to refuse this person, so she was hiding out someplace until the whole thing blew over. Her friend thinks she may be in serious trouble."

Or her troubles could all be over, McGuffin thought. "What makes you think I'm the private detective this person wanted her to talk to?" he asked.

"Tanya told her she had to get away because she didn't want anybody planting a bomb on her car. Knowing you're looking for the guy who tried to blow up Victor, I didn't have to be Sherlock Holmes to come up with your name. You aren't going to deny it, are you?"

"You've got the right man," McGuffin allowed. But that was all he would allow. "I heard she was a friend of Angelo Tieri's, so I put the word out that I'd like to ask her a few questions. But I never heard from her." McGuffin shrugged indifferently. "It was nothing important, just part of the routine investigation."

"Well, there's nothing routine about it anymore," Strauss said. "You've stirred up somebody and now Tanya's life may be in danger."

"I'm sorry about that," McGuffin said. "But homicide is a contact sport. Anybody who plays is liable to get hurt."

"But Tanya's not a player," Strauss reminded him.

"Then why is she hiding?" Or worse, he thought. "Your girlfriend is part of the plot to kill my client, and the fact that she's your girlfriend doesn't make you look too good either."

"That's a very serious accusation."

111

"Slander's the least of my worries," McGuffin replied. "Tanya knows who tried to kill my client, and if I can find her I can wrap this case up. You on the other hand want her back for your own reasons, so I suggest we put our heads together."

"Why should I help you?" Strauss asked.

"Because," McGuffin said, leaning across the table, "she's betrayed a murderer. If I don't get to her before he does, he'll kill her. So tell me, who introduced you to Tanya?"

"I told you, I met her at the—"

"Yeah, but who arranged it? Who fixed you up with her?"

"Nobody fixed me up," he replied testily. "I was at the club with Conrad Daniels and he—"

"Conrad Daniels," McGuffin interrupted. "He introduced you to Tanya."

"But he did not fix me up."

"Call it what you like. To me it's a quid pro quo. You give Daniels bags of money and he gives you girls."

"That's not the way it is," he protested.

"Before you put a downpayment on the cottage with the picket fence, you should know that Daniels has passed Tanya around to a few of his friends, including Angelo Tieri."

"Angelo?"

"She never mentioned him?"

"Never."

"What about Johnny Belmont?"

"Him too?"

"She had a busy calendar," McGuffin said.

"I don't care, I want you to find her," Laird Strauss said.

McGuffin climbed to his feet. "I wish I could believe that," he said, then turned and left the coffeeshop.

The morning sun gave way to a dull sky as he drove north on the Taconic Parkway, then changed to the color of plums as he climbed the hills past Yorktown Heights. A few minutes later the first large drop of rain slammed against the windshield, celebrated by an orange gash and a blast of

112

thunder that shook the car. McGuffin switched the head-
lights on and backed off the pedal as the rain leapt at him in
a blinding silver sheet.

There was no red Ferrari parked in front, nor was there
any light coming from Johnny's cottage when McGuffin
drew to a stop on the flooded drive. There were two cars in
the courtyard, pressed up close to the service door, as if
seeking shelter from the wind-whipped rain. There were
lights in the kitchen and an upstairs bedroom, but McGuffin
could see no one moving about inside the main house. He
took a deep breath, pushed the car door open and sprinted
for the service porch. He pounded on the door until a
moment later it was opened by a white-haired woman in a
black dress. McGuffin introduced himself, reminding her
that he had visited Johnny several days earlier and, like her,
was an employee of Victor Belmont. She said her name was
Mrs. Cummings and they were pleased to have the company.

"I saw a light upstairs," McGuffin said.

"That was Mr. Cummings trying to stop up the window,"
she said, as a thin bald man entered, rolling down his white
sleeves.

"Every time we get rain from the north that darned
window leaks," he said.

"Maybe I'd better have a look at it," McGuffin said,
starting in the direction from which Mr. Cummings had just
come. The older man caught him in the foyer, switched on
the chandelier and led him up the stairs. McGuffin glanced
in each of the rooms as he made his way down the hall,
while Mr. Cummings waited outside the leaking bedroom.
"Just wanted to if see the others were tight," McGuffin
explained, as he stepped past him. The room was empty and
a puddle of water had collected on the floor, despite several
towels stuffed around the sash. "Yeah, it's leaking," McGuffin
said, then turned and walked out of the room. He examined
the entire house and basement while the caretaker followed,
puzzled but silent.

"What about Johnny's house?" McGuffin asked, when
they returned to the kitchen.

113

"That one's tight as a drum."

"Just the same I'd better have a look."

Mr. Cummings gave him a key from the pegboard beside the kitchen door but made no offer to accompany him. Mrs. Cummings offered him the raincoat hanging beside the door and, holding it over his head, McGuffin dashed across the courtyard to the front door. He found the light switch inside the door and the furnishings unchanged. He called Tanya's name as he poked among the cold rooms, but he saw or heard nothing to indicate anyone had recently been there. Satisfied, he pulled the raincoat over his head and sprinted back to the main house.

"I take it you and Mrs. Cummings were here on the night of the explosion," McGuffin said, as he returned the key to the pegboard.

"Yes, sir, we sure were."

"Can you tell me if Johnny Belmont had a guest in his cottage that night?"

The caretaker exchanged a confused look with his wife before replying "No, sir, he was alone."

"If you knew that Mr. Belmont had brought a woman home with him that evening, someone other than his wife, would you have told the police?"

"I don't know about that, but I do know Mr. Belmont was alone that night. I'm positive."

"How can you be so sure?"

"I got eyes, ain't I?" the old man answered.

"Yes, sir, you do," McGuffin acknowledged. "But were they open when Johnny arrived in the middle of the night?"

Again he exchanged a look with his wife before shaking his head slowly. "I wasn't awake when he got here, if that's what you mean."

"That's what I mean," McGuffin said. "And after Johnny was taken to the hospital, did you and Mrs. Cummings remain here at the house?"

"Yes, sir, we did," he answered.

"Except for when you drove me to the hospital," his wife reminded him.

"That's right, we was gone for maybe a coupla hours the next morning," he answered.

"Do you remember where Johnny's red car was when you left for the hospital?"

"Right in front of the cottage where he always leaves it," Mrs. Cummings answered—just one more thing, like his dirty socks and underwear.

"And where was it when you got back?"

"The same place," the housekeeper replied firmly.

"Say, just what kinda work is it you do for Mr. Belmont anyway?" Mr. Cummings asked.

"I'm a PI," McGuffin answered.

"PI?"

"Property inspector."

"Aha," he said. "Then I guess you want to have a look at the garage."

"Another time," McGuffin said, then thanked them and ran for his car.

As he circled in front of the house and started down the long tree-lined drive, he remembered Johnny's new house, stopped and backed up. A newly made drive spoking off the circle and through the trees to the left of the cottage led up and around the back of the lake, affording a few glimpses of the churning, rain-splattered water below, and ended in a loop at the front of the house.

McGuffin dashed the short distance to the front door of the concrete pill box (the architect's skill was only visible from the lake) and pressed the buzzer. He waited, rang again, then tried the door. It was open. A flash of lightning over the lake illuminated the room briefly. Furniture and cartons were strewn randomly about the large room, while on the concrete deck beyond the broad glass wall, raindrops danced and sang to be admitted. Beyond this the clouds and lake and rain merged vaguely in the distance like a Turner, churned by thunder and lightning.

He found a bank of light switches and turned them all on, then went from level to level, searching for Tanya. Only the furniture in the open spaces suggested the room's function—a

115

bed here, a dining table there, all waiting to be arranged by Penny Belmont and her interior decorator.

The last bedroom on the bottom floor, however, had already been arranged for living. Teak chests and a dressing table had been carefully arranged along one wall, along with a large bed against the opposite wall. A down comforter covered the bare mattress, but a pile of sheets lay on the floor at the foot of the bed. There were six empty clothes hangers in the closet and an empty tampon box in the bathroom wastebasket. There had been a woman here, and when McGuffin found a quite large bra in the laundry pile at the foot of the bed, he was reasonably certain it was Tanya.

It was McGuffin's idea to include Johnny. Victor knew nothing about it until the houseman announced that he was in the lobby.

"I want him to hear this," McGuffin said. He was seated on the tufted leather couch in Victor's snug library, his spiral notebook open on his knee.

"Send him up," Victor said uncertainly into the intercom. "I hope you know what you're doing," he said, crossing to the cocktail table.

So do I, McGuffin thought, as he watched Victor toss two ice cubes into his glass, followed by a generous splash of Black Label. At a particularly loud clap of thunder, Victor's hand shook, rattling the ice in his glass. He flicked a smile at McGuffin, then walked across the library to the rain-lashed window, daring the lightning to strike him. The storm had followed McGuffin south and was now going into its second night. The mayor said it was welcome after the summer drought, but the man in the flooded street wasn't so sure it was a good thing. Subways and buses were running irregularly, the cabs had floated away, and part of the city was without electricity.

Johnny Belmont entered the room still wearing a wet raincoat. He shook hands with his brother and McGuffin, then commented needlessly on the weather as he removed

116

and handed his coat to the houseman. When he was seated expectantly in a plaid wing chair with a drink, McGuffin began.

"Antonia Ruiz has disappeared," he announced.

"Don't you think I know that?" Johnny asked, uncrossing his legs.

"I'm sorry—" Victor began.

"Tanya," McGuffin explained. "Johnny's mistress." Victor frowned disapprovingly at his little brother as McGuffin went on. "Johnny says she was with him on the night of the explosion."

"She was," Johnny said.

"But on the night of the explosion, Mr. and Mrs. Cummings and your brother and his wife all say you were alone."

"Because I didn't want them to know—I told you."

"I know, you sneaked her in. But how did she get back to New York while you were lying in a hospital bed?"

"How—? I don't know, she must have taken my car."

"Mrs. Cummings says your car never left the drive."

"That's right," Victor said. "Your car was there until the day you got back from the hospital."

"Hey, what is this—let's all get Johnny?"

"Of course not," Victor answered. "We just want to know how this woman could have gotten back to New York."

"Maybe she took a cab to the village and got a train—I don't know. I was in the hospital, under sedation, suffering from shock. Do you think I was worrying about how my date got home?"

"But when you were out of the hospital and no longer suffering from shock, weren't you concerned enough then to ask how she got home?"

"I really wasn't worried about it."

"In all fairness to Johnny, it would be like him not to worry," Victor assured McGuffin.

"Thank you," Johnny said.

"What's happened to Tanya?" McGuffin demanded.

"Why are you asking me?"

"Did she refuse to talk to me, or did she refuse to lie for you?"

"Neither. She was all set to tell you she was with me that night, and anything else you wanted to know. Then she just disappeared."

"That seems a bit excessive. If she didn't want to talk to me she didn't have to, I can't force her. Or is it possible somebody else didn't want her to talk to me?"

"Who?" Johnny asked.

"Whoever sent Angelo to plant the bomb on Victor's car."

"And who is that?" Victor demanded. "If you know something, tell us and stop beating around the bush."

"Let's begin with the person who has the strongest motive," McGuffin suggested, as he climbed to his feet. "I don't want either of you to take this personally, but that person, Johnny, is you."

"What! You're crazy," Johnny said.

"Amos, I don't want this," Victor Belmont said.

"Objectively," McGuffin said, raising a hand to silence his client, pleading for a little rope. "If you had been blown up that night, your little brother would now be the sole manager of the Belmont Organization. He'd be able to reorganize the company, pay himself a big dividend and get Tony Pliers off his back."

"Tony Pliers?"

McGuffin identified Tony Pliers for his client and informed him of Johnny's debt to Gregory Scott, the society bookmaker.

"Johnny, when are you going to learn?" Victor asked.

"Is it my fault I don't have any money?" Johnny asked. "You're the one who threw me off the board and stopped my dividends."

"And it was just because of this sort of thing that you forced me to do it," Victor responded.

"I'm not asking for money to pay my bookie, I'm only asking for what's mine. And don't tell me about the house, because I can't pay bills with a house. I need cash."

"Why don't *you* tell me about the house?" McGuffin suggested. "Did Victor tell you to charge the house to the company?"

"You know he did—I told you."

"Johnny, where did you ever get an idea like that?" Victor asked. "That's not true and you know it."

"Vic, what are you saying?" Johnny asked, jumping to his feet. "We sat right here in this room and you told me! You told me things were gonna be tight for a while but I should build this house and expense it to the company."

"There must be some misunderstanding here, Johnny. I never understood why you wanted a second house at all."

"You told me you wanted Penny and me to have a place to entertain clients!" he fairly wailed.

"Johnny, how often have we entertained clients at the compound? I've had a few people up for a quiet weekend on rare occasions, but that's it. The place is a retreat, not a place to entertain."

"But you told me you wanted to change that. You told me we'd need a big house," he insisted.

Victor regarded his brother with a pained look. "I have no idea where you could have gotten such an idea."

"Victor, I didn't imagine this," Johnny insisted.

"Are there any witnesses to this agreement?" McGuffin asked both of them.

"Yeah—I mean, Penny knows, I told her—"

"There can be no witnesses to a nonevent," Victor said.

"Of course there were no strangers who witnessed it," Johnny said. "What we were doing was defrauding the IRS."

"Speak for yourself," Victor said. "And for your own protection I'd advise you to say no more about this. Let's move on," he said, swiveling to McGuffin.

"No, let's hold it right there," Johnny said, stalking across the room. He stopped in front of the desk, a bulwark from behind which Victor orchestrated the discussion from his swivel chair. "You're accusing me of embezzling funds and I want it cleared up now."

119

"I've been going over it with my tax attorney—we're trying to find a way to straighten it out—so if you'd like to be of any help, you'll never again discuss it in the presence of anyone else. Is that understood?"

"You're trying to make this look like it was my idea."

"Johnny, please, we'll discuss this later," Victor said, pointing a finger at his little brother.

"Okay—okay," he said.

Victor waited until he had backed across the room and settled back in his chair, then swiveled to McGuffin. "Do you have something more?"

McGuffin nodded and flipped to the next page of his notebook. "I went to the village and talked to both of the cab drivers. Neither one of them came to the house on the day of the explosion, and neither of them saw a woman of Tanya's distinctive anatomical description. So if Tanya didn't leave in your car, or didn't leave in a cab, how did she leave your cottage?"

"I give up, how did she?" Johnny asked sullenly.

McGuffin turned his back on him and spoke to Victor. "The police didn't find another car near the house, leading them to conclude naturally that Angelo had an accomplice, somebody who drove him to the house and waited to take him back. Then when the bomb went off the driver split. I didn't have any trouble with that until the day I drove up to your house. Finding it was like finding the source of the Nile. Whoever drove Angelo Tieri up there that night almost certainly had to have been there before."

"You found it by yourself," Johnny reminded him.

McGuffin turned to him. "In the middle of the day, with a carefully drawn map."

"You did it, it can't be that hard," Johnny insisted.

"No, it's not impossible," McGuffin said. "But neither was it necessary. Not when the bomber had a guide."

"Just what are you saying, McGuffin?" Johnny demanded.

"I'm saying it was Tanya who drove Angelo Tieri to the house that night. No one saw her enter the house because she didn't. You led the way in your car, Tanya and Angelo followed in hers."

120

"You're full of shit!"

"Be quiet," Victor instructed.

"She waited in the car at the head of the drive while Angelo carried the bomb to the garage, where you were waiting for him," McGuffin went on. "With two black Mercedes Benzes in the garage, you wanted to be damned sure Angelo wired the right one. You sent him into the garage and waited in the drive for him to finish. That's why you were there when the bomb went off, not because you heard someone in the garage and went to investigate."

"He's making this all up!" Johnny shouted, charging once more to his feet. "There's not a bit of truth in any of it!"

"If there's no truth in it, it can't hurt you," Victor replied.

"You know I'd never do such a thing, Vic! We may have had our differences, but we're brothers, for Christ's sake!"

"I'm sorry if this disturbs you, Johnny, but I would like to hear everything Amos has to say. Continue," he instructed.

Muttering innocence and incredulity, Johnny Belmont repaired to the farthest corner of the room while McGuffin went on.

"What happened after that was to be expected. When Tanya heard the bomb go off, she realized her passenger wasn't coming back, so she deadheaded it into New York. That's why the police never found Angelo Tieri's car at the scene of the crime."

"It's not true, she was with me," Johnny recited softly from the back of the room. "She'll tell you."

"It's a tidy supposition," Victor said after a moment. "But again, in all fairness to my brother, lacking this girl's testimony it's only speculation."

McGuffin stuffed his hands in his pockets, looked at the floor and nodded. "Oddly enough it's Tanya's absence that lends a presumption of truth to the speculation. Johnny had no need for a witness. He could say he went outside to investigate an intruder, which was why he was standing near the garage when the bomb went off, and nobody's going to question it. The police didn't. But Johnny still had a guilty conscience, and consequently a shaky set of nerves. John-

ny's a hunter, he's got a houseful of guns and he knows how to use them. Yet he went out to investigate an intruder without taking a gun along."

"So what?" Johnny demanded. "That doesn't prove a damned thing."

"True," McGuffin allowed. "But it was a weakness in your alibi and you recognized it the moment I brought it up. And it made you jumpy. Enough so that you felt the need to overcome my suspicion. And that's why you overreacted. Until then the fact that you were awake at three-thirty in the morning hadn't seemed any more important than forgetting the gun, but now it required an explanation. Then when I voiced suspicion that a social animal like you would go up there alone in the middle of the night, you got scared. There was no need for it, I could only speculate at that point, I couldn't prove a thing.

"But that wasn't good enough. You wanted to prove to me that you were innocent so you decided to produce a witness to clear you. You decided then and there—you had never discussed it with her before—that Tanya would be your witness. You chose her because she was already involved—you knew she couldn't refuse to help. But you overreacted, Johnny. And you also overestimated Tanya's commitment. She was willing to drive Angelo to your house and drive him home again. But she was not going to admit she had been there, nor would she submit to my interrogation. But you were insistent. You told her you had already told me she was there, so she did the only reasonable thing—she fled."

"Tanya was with me," Johnny insisted dully.

"In bed with you?"

"Yes."

"That's not very likely, Johnny. Tanya was Angelo Tieri's mistress, not yours. She was in love with him, she was planning to marry him."

"You're crazy! Who told you that?"

"A friend of hers, it doesn't matter who. What matters is you made another mistake. You claimed Tanya was your

122

mistress when in fact she was just your business associate, like Angelo. The two of you pretended to be lovers just to make it appear unlikely that Angelo was part of your conspiracy."

"That's not true, Tanya's in love with me," Johnny insisted.

"So much so that she ran off after you were injured?"

"She didn't!" Johnny shouted. McGuffin and Victor waited for an explanation. "I mean she didn't leave me—she loves me," he added.

"It's true, she didn't exactly run off," McGuffin said. "You hid her out at your new house after she refused to talk to me. You realized she was scared and unreliable, so you had to put her on ice for a while. Isn't that true, Johnny?"

"I don't know what you're talking about."

"I'm talking about this," McGuffin said, pulling the large bra from his pocket. He tossed it in the air and Johnny caught it neatly with one hand. "I found it in the bedroom of the new house. Recognize it?"

"This could belong to anybody," he said, examining it.

"Scarcely anybody," McGuffin said.

"Okay, maybe it's Tanya's, so what?" he asked, with an easy shrug. "Tanya and I spent a couple of nights there, just for a little variety. But that was before the bomb, not after."

"You're quick on your feet," McGuffin said. "But I think you're lying through your teeth."

"Then prove it. Prove it or shut up, goddammit! Because all you've done so far is make vicious charges about me that aren't true."

"Johnny, this isn't a court of law," Victor said in a soothing voice. "I'm not trying to indict or convict you of anything, but I will know the truth. I think you owe me at least that."

"Owe you? That's very funny, Victor, very funny. Just what the hell do I owe you?"

"Well, I have made you a rather wealthy man," Victor began.

123

"That's bullshit! I'm wealthy because our father left us a fortune!"

"That's hardly fair, Johnny. I've worked hard, I've increased the business enormously."

"You've done a good job and you did it all by yourself, I won't argue about that," Johnny replied. "But that was the way you wanted it. I tried to help but you did everything you could to cut me out of the business."

"Johnny, that's not true. I tried to include you, but everything you did turned sour. Your projects cost us millions of dollars."

"Because you sabotaged them."

"Sabotaged my own company?" Victor asked.

"Exactly. You were willing to destroy my projects and lose millions if it would discredit me and keep me off the board. Ever since I came into the company you've been painting me as an irresponsible playboy."

"Johnny, Johnny—" Victor said, shaking his head slowly from side to side. "You're upset. I can understand that, and I'm sorry. But if you felt that I was taking you away from commerce and forcing you to be a playboy, why didn't you say something to me before this?"

Johnny's laugh was a short derisive burst. "You're very good with words, Vic. That's why I didn't say anything before," he told McGuffin. "Your client is a conjurer. He can make you see what he wants you to see and not see what he doesn't want you to see. He can destroy you at the bargaining table and make you his friend for life. Or his brother. I stopped complaining years ago," he said, turning back to Victor. "Because every time I did I came away with a little less. And that's why, when he said he wanted to reorganize the company, I said go ahead. And that's why, when he told me to build a house, I did. I just wanted to keep him happy and keep what I had. But I was still asking too much. He wants it all and he'll get it, even if it means sending me to jail for something I didn't do."

"Nobody's going to send you to jail for something you didn't do," McGuffin assured him, before Victor could re-

124

ply. "But you will be punished for what you did do, there's no way around that. And your punishment will depend upon just how culpable you are. If you planned this alone, your responsibility is great and the penalty will be severe. But if you were persuaded to do this by someone else, and you were to tell me who that person is, then in that case the greater blame might shift from you to him. There was someone else involved, isn't that true, Johnny?"

"I don't know anything about it," Johnny answered in a weary voice.

"I think it would be much better if you were to tell us everything," Victor prodded gently.

"I'll bet you do," Johnny said. "You'd love to see me confess all and go to jail and leave everything to you."

"Johnny, we're talking about something far more serious than your half of the business. If I wanted you out, your embezzlement of company funds is already more than sufficient for that."

"You told me to—"

"But that's not what I want," Victor interrupted. "I just want to clear this thing up and put it behind us. I want you to tell me what happened and I give you my word, I'll do everything I can to protect you."

"Your brother is right, Johnny," McGuffin added. "You can either talk to him or the district attorney."

"Uh-uh," Johnny said, turning his head slowly from side to side. "I don't have to talk to anybody because you've got nothing."

McGuffin watched silently as Johnny Belmont made his exit. The kid was right, he had nothing. He was frustrated and he was angry. Until he remembered something his old boss, Miles Dwindling, had once told him: "Every case has its own rhythm. Rush it and you lose it."

Chapter 15

McGuffin sat watching the fish in the wall-enclosed aquarium behind the receptionist, while he waited for Andre Hersh to see him. There were a few dozen of them skittering around behind the glass, all a dull brown and no more than a couple of inches long. Although the fish were dull, the things lying on the bottom of the tank were most curious—a human skull and a gold Rolex watch, encircling the ulna and radius bones of an arm.

"What kind of fish are those?" McGuffin asked the receptionist.

"Piranhas," she answered, as she reached for the phone. Mr. Hersh would see him now.

Hersh apologized for keeping him waiting and McGuffin assured him it was all right. "Those bones in your piranha tank," he said, pulling the antique French chair up to the desk, "are they real?"

The lawyer's vest jiggled when he laughed. "Most people want to know if the Rolex is real—which speaks well for you, Amos. The answer is, they're both real."

Hersh rapped his knuckles once on McGuffin's file and said, "I got the PI report on your ex and it's not good. Or rather it's good and that's bad. In fact, I put the slimiest divorce investigator I could find on this case and he came away so impressed by this woman that he decided to get into another line of work."

"So what are you saying?" McGuffin asked. "That's it's a hopeless case?"

"No," Hersh answered, checking to see that his last few strands of hair were in place. "I'm saying we gotta find an even slimier investigator."

"Forget it," McGuffin said.

"You want her back, don't you?"

"Not that way."

"Amos, there is no other way, trust me. She's got Hilda, we're going to the mat on this. You seen Hilda? Big," he said, stretching his hands over his head. "Her diet consists entirely of unprepared Jewish male lawyers—the bones, the Rolex, the whole megilla."

"You don't have to worry," McGuffin said, getting to his feet. "I'm withdrawing my complaint."

"Withdraw! Amos, my clients don't withdraw. I've got a reputation to uphold."

"And I have a relationship with my daughter that I have to uphold."

"Amos, wait," he pleaded, as his secretary broke in on the intercom. "Not now!"

"It's very important!" she shouted in an excited voice.

"What's so important for God's sake?"

"Franz Tutin's theater is on fire!"

While they crept across town in a cab, Andre explained why Franz Tutin had phoned him with the information that his theater was on fire. "It's the boy scout in me. I represent the Actors Company for free so I shouldn't feel guilty about tearing the throat out of rich husbands. Driver, can you go a little faster? And the answer is yes, we're going to a fire."

"Do you and Victor support all the same charities?" McGuffin asked.

"Just a coincidence," Hersh said.

They got out at the barricade at the head of the block and plunged into the crowd. Police cars and fire engines filled the street and hoses climbed up the church stairs and through the open doors, reaching deep into the back of the building where the fire burned. McGuffin and Andre pushed and slid through the crowd until they emerged in front of a fireman who stopped their forward progress. Hersh told him he was the lawyer for the Actors Company, but the firefighter wasn't impressed.

"This is a fire, not a car accident," he said.

Across the street, against a background of billowing smoke, Franz Tutin was surrounded by a crew from Channel 2. Seeing Hersh, he broke away and sloshed across the flooded street while the crew followed, hoping for more information.

"You told me you had vorked things out vit the union!" he shouted.

"I thought I had."

"Then vat do you call this?"

Smelling blood, the reporter from Channel 2, a woman in a trench coat, leaned in and asked, "Are you saying that this fire was set by union dissidents?"

"He's not saying anything like that," Hersh said, pulling Franz away from the reporter.

"But there has been union unrest at the Actors Company, has there not?" she called futilely, as her subject was swallowed up by the crowd.

Hersh led Tutin to the French restaurant a few doors away and stopped under the tricolored canopy. "What happened? Did you see anyone?"

"I saw smoke, that's all! Vhen I opened the door I smelled it, from under the main stage, in the dressing rooms—I don't know! I called the fire department then I called you!"

"Take it easy," Hersh said, patting his client's hand.

Franz Tutin spluttered angrily while his theater burned, insisting that he was rational and that someone was out to deliberately destroy the Actors Company. "I am Stanislavski's sole heir!" he cried. "All the others are imposters! They think they can burn me out, but they vill never stop me! Never!" Then he turned to his attorney and inquired in a calm voice, "Who is our insurance man?"

"I'll get in touch with him," Hersh promised. "You just take it easy."

128

"I'm fine, I'm fine," Franz Tutin said, staring across his lawyer's bald head at the smoke issuing from the church tower. "My beautiful theater," he repeated softly over and over again, until it began to resemble a religious litany. When the tears broke and ran down his pink cheeks, Hersh stretched to put an arm around his shoulder and murmur reassuringly to him. He thanked God that no one had been inside and assured him that the building could be rebuilt, but the words fell on deaf ears.

Franz Tutin's theater was not just a building, it was the symbol and culmination of the work of a lifetime, and now it was all going up in fire and smoke. In a short while theatrical pundits the world over would begin expressing their feelings at the loss of this hallowed institution. To McGuffin, standing beside the bleary-eyed director, it offered the hope that Marilyn might reconsider her plan to remain in New York.

The effect on the world of arts and letters to the burning of the Actors Company theater was more far-reaching than McGuffin could have anticipated. There were those who likened the fiery loss to Stonehenge. "Although the stones remain, something of the meaning is forever lost," a TV sitcom star wrote from Hollywood, while a less enamored New York critic lamented only that the custom of the sea, that the captain go down with his ship, did not obtain in the theater.

That Franz Tutin would not go down was brought home to McGuffin when he was summoned to a meeting by the director himself. They met in a dank, charred-smelling office behind the ticket booth in the front of the theater.

"This is the part of the theater least damaged by the fire," Franz Tutin said as they settled themselves in folding chairs. McGuffin, who had not seen Franz since the day of the fire earlier in the week, coughed and assured him that he was comfortable. Franz inquired after Marilyn and McGuffin assured him she was behind him 100 percent, which was sadly true. What McGuffin viewed as a clear direction from

129

heaven that they should return post haste to San Francisco was to Marilyn an equally clear test of her dedication to the the theater.

"Even if I wished to give up my own career, I could never desert Franz at a time like this," she had told McGuffin in the tiny kitchen of her Greenwich Village sublet—a far, far better thing that I do than anything I have ever done speech, delivered with everything but the back of the hand to the forehead. Tutin had at least taught her some restraint.

"You're a detective," Franz Tutin said.

"Private," McGuffin qualified.

"If there is dirty vork afoot, you seek it out. Vere there is darkness and mystery, you bring light."

"I wouldn't put it that way on my curriculum vitae, but yes, I sometimes do those things. Why do you ask?"

"Because I require your services."

"I see," McGuffin replied. "You want someone to find out who torched the place."

"No," the director said, shaking his head. "The fire is merely the final straw. Someone has been trying for more than a year to get me out of my theater. Last fall a stone fell from the belfry, very nearly striking one of the audience during the intermission of *St. Joan.* During the vinter vandals broke the boiler, and during the summer they broke the air-conditioning. Later ve vere plagued by strikes, and now finally ve are burned out. Someone, Mr. McGuffin, is trying to destroy the Actors Company."

"That does seem to be a lot of bad luck in one year," McGuffin conceded. "But that might be all it is, just bad luck. Apparently the arson squad can't even be sure it's arson."

"That's true," the director admitted. "And I might agree vit you if it veren't for this," he said, extracting an envelope from inside his blue blazer.

He removed the letter from the envelope and handed it to McGuffin. It was from a realty company offering to purchase the Actors Company theater for an amount "considerably in excess of its present salvage value."

130

"A messenger delivered that the day after the fire. It is the same company that has been after me all year to sell. I vould have thrown it away, just as I did the others, except for what Andre Hersh told me that morning."

"What did Andre tell you?"

"That the fire insurance on the theater has expired. There is no insurance, ve have no money to repair the damage to my theater."

"I don't understand," McGuffin said. "The insurance company must have sent you some notice that they were going to cancel."

"They claim they informed Andre's office, but he says he knows nothing about it. I have been over it until I am sick, Mr. McGuffin, there is no insurance. I don't know how Andre could have allowed something like this to happen, but he has."

"All right, all right," McGuffin said, bouncing the folded letter off one hand. "Does Hersh know anything about this?"

"I read it to him over the phone. He doesn't know anything about it, but—maybe . . ." His voice trailed off as he shrugged.

"Maybe what?"

"He said maybe I should think of selling."

"And would you?"

"Never. I vill rebuild the theater even if it kills me."

That was a distinct possibility, McGuffin knew. "Okay, I'll help you," he said.

A phone call to the RVS Realty Corporation was, as McGuffin had known it would be, unfruitful. Yes, they represented a buyer interested in the Actors Company property, but no, they would not disclose his identity. No matter, McGuffin knew where such secrets were kept.

Laird Strauss was at first unwilling to cooperate, as McGuffin knew he would be. However, when he learned that the information McGuffin was after might prove detri-

131

mental to his nemesis, Victor Belmont, as well as beneficial to himself, he was helpless to refuse.

McGuffin stood before the green screen in Stauss's office while Strauss relayed his instructions to the operator hunched over the keyboard. A moment after McGuffin had identified the block, a graphic representation of its buildings, including the recently burned church, appeared on the screen.

"Let's start with the theater," McGuffin said.

The operator punched a button and a list of names, dates and prices appeared.

"It was purchased by Franz Tutin twenty years ago for fifteen thousand dollars and there hasn't been any activity since," Strauss explained.

"Let's try the one next to it," McGuffin proposed.

Again the operator punched a key and Strauss interpreted the data. "The building was sold last February for seven hundred fifty thousand dollars to an EOD Corporation."

"Can that machine tell me who the principals of the EOD Corporation are?" McGuffin asked, as a moment later three names appeared on the screen. None were familiar.

"That doesn't mean much," Strauss said. "Those people could be officers of the corporation and not even know it. Find the attorney who represented the buyer," he instructed. The operator pressed a key and the name of the buyer's attorney appeared on the screen.

"Andre Hersh," McGuffin read aloud.

"Know him?"

"He's handling a domestic relations case for me."

"An odd coincidence," Strauss said.

"That's what he said," McGuffin remembered. "Next building."

The next building too had been sold within the last year, to a corporation with different initials, but again represented by Andre Hersh. The computer moved down the block from building to building with the same result.

"There's a bombed-out block a couple of blocks from there," McGuffin said. He described it and watched the screen as the operator roved over the neighborhood with his

132

aerial camera. "That's it!" McGuffin said, halting him at the blighted block of mostly unoccupied buildings where McGuffin had earlier met the mayor of New York City. Again most of the buildings were owned by a similar collection of acronymous corporations, all of them represented by Andre Hersh.

"It looks like your domestic relations lawyer is into real estate in a big way," Strauss observed.

"Not without the theater," McGuffin replied.

"True," Laird Strauss said, licking his lips.

Chapter 16

Victor Belmont and a woman were swimming laps when McGuffin pushed past the houseman and into the pool room. The houseman began to apologize until Victor, treading water in the middle of the pool, told him it was all right. It was not until the woman climbed the ladder at the deep end of the pool that McGuffin realized they were both naked.

"You haven't met my wife," Victor gasped. "Kay Belmont, Amos McGuffin."

"How do you do?" she said, turning to the detective.

"Nice to see you," McGuffin said.

She smiled, then turned and walked gracefully across the tiles, snatching a white robe from the bench and trailing it through the door after her. Victor swam for the side and sprang out of the pool in a powerful, watery thrust. He was apparently not as impressed with his wife as McGuffin was.

"So what's this all about, have you discovered something new?" he asked, as he briskly toweled himself dry.

"Yeah, I've discovered something new, but it's not about Johnny," McGuffin replied. "It's about that block in Hell's Kitchen, the one you have no financial interest in. The one you were going to fix up for nothing, just to give something back to this wonderful city that's given so much to you."

"But I don't own that block," Victor replied calmly.

"I know, it's owned by the ABC, XYZ, Tweedle dum tweedle dee corporations, but we both know who they are, so let's not split hairs."

134

Victor considered for a moment, decided further lies were useless, then nodded. "Okay, I own most of that block."

"And you also own most of Franz Tutin's block. Except for the theater because Franz won't sell it. Only now that it was burned and Andre Hersh conveniently forgot to pay the insurance premiums, you think it might come up for sale, and at a very good price."

"You aren't implying that I had something to do with that fire, or Andre's lapse, are you?" Victor asked, turning his back to McGuffin.

"No, I'm not implying," McGuffin said, following him along the edge of the pool. "When Hersh's firm is the one you used for all your real estate closings and when you placed Hersh in the Actors Company; and when you lied to me about your plans for the neighborhood—I'm not implying, I'm accusing." Victor continued to walk and McGuffin continued to follow. At the bench at the deep end of the pool, Victor calmly picked up the remaining white robe and slipped it on. "Your little brother may be no better than you, but he's right about one thing. There is no limit to your greed. You'll invite addicts into your buildings, hire thugs to frighten the tenants out, destroy the heating systems, cut off the water—you'll even commit arson and possibly murder."

Victor Belmont pulled the terry-cloth hood over his head and turned to McGuffin. "Are you finished?" he asked.

"Totally," McGuffin said, then turned and started for the door.

"Aren't you going to let me say anything in my defense?" The words echoed hollowly in the tiled room.

"You lied once too often," McGuffin called without breaking stride.

"I only lied to save you from something you couldn't understand."

In spite of himself, McGuffin had to stop, had to know what Victor Belmont knew that he couldn't. "Try me," he said.

Belmont stuffed his hands in the large pockets of his robe, then motioned with his head for McGuffin to follow. "I want to show you something," he said.

McGuffin followed him through the glass doors, out onto the deck, through the planted garden to the rail at the edge of the roof. The sun had set, but the reflected glow of the city would hold back the darkness until some great calamity occurred, Armageddon or another blackout. From this side of the roof they could see the great buildings stretching to the East River, spanned by the Fifty-ninth Street Bridge and the aerial tram stretching to Roosevelt Island.

"I've lived in New York all my life and seen all the great cities of the world, but I never cease to be amazed by Manhattan Island," Victor Belmont said, while looking down at the traffic on Third Avenue.

"And for every light there's a broken heart," McGuffin recited.

"And cynicism is the plague of our time," Victor Belmont rejoined. "The mad, the homeless and the criminals are allowed to wander those streets, offending or injuring decent people almost at will, while people like you and me pay our taxes and go to church. We wouldn't so much as dream of throwing a piece of paper on the sidewalk, while the poor shit in the alley and nobody does anything about it."

"What would you do, sweep them out of the city?" McGuffin asked.

Victor turned to McGuffin with a pleased smile. "Exactly."

"That doesn't solve the problem, it just pushes it somewhere else."

"I have a plan for the poor as well," Victor assured him. "But for the moment just listen to my plan for Manhattan with an open mind."

McGuffin promised he would and Victor Belmont's radical ideas spewed out like a mad FAX. To the rest of the world, Manhattan with its skyscrapers, the Statue of Liberty and the Brooklyn Bridge symbolized America. It was a hallowed place deserving of preferential treatment, a special preserve where art and commerce should flower to their fullest, and anything standing in the way should be swept aside. Ghettoes should be bulldozed and their inhabitants relocated to Brooklyn, Queens, the Bronx and Staten Island. And in their place parks, gardens, concert halls, libraries, monorails and skyscrapers would be built. Manhattan would become the ultimate city, the Athenian ideal.

"It seems to me you might have a problem selling it to the voters," McGuffin commented lazily after Victor had presented his vision of the future.

"Yes, there's the rub," he replied sadly. "Even though the mayor shares my vision, he knows that to say so publicly would mean his defeat. So I'm forced to resort to subterfuge if I'm to get my projects done. I lied to you because I knew you'd take the side of the tenants. But when the tenants are relocated and a beautiful new building stands on that block, then you'll see the virtue in what I'm doing."

"And how many tenants have you relocated so far?"

Victor opened his mouth and closed it. "Some people would rather fight."

"And Franz Tutin is one of them. He's hired me to find out who tried to burn him out," McGuffin informed his client.

"I can't see that your business with Franz has anything to do with mine," he answered.

"That's very sporting of you," McGuffin said. "But I have to warn you, after I nail the guy who killed Nina Tieri, I'm going to go after the guy who torched the church," he said, then turned and, without saying good-bye or shaking his client's hand, left.

Except for his professional pride, McGuffin no longer cared if Johnny Belmont were to kill his client. Each in his own way was equally despicable—Victor a half-mad brigand posing as a social revolutionary, Johnny a rich but worthless young punk. If now that the activities of the Actors Company had been suspended, Marilyn was willing to return to San Francisco, he might even be willing to abandon a case for the first time in his life and go home. Unfortunately Marilyn was not inclined to give up New York or her career over a fire, unless accompanied by war, famine, pestilence and death. Even though the theater was closed she was busier than ever, auditioning for other producers during the day and working on an Actors Company benefit in the evenings. Franz Tutin was resolved, especially after learning from McGuffin that Victor Belmont was probably the man behind the fire, to rebuild his theater, and the artistic community, including many of his Hollywood luminaries, was rallying to his support—which could only cause Victor Belmont some considerable distress.

McGuffin realized that helping Franz Tutin was scarcely the way to get Marilyn back to San Francisco, but he was the victim of principle. He remained convinced that Tutin was a charlatan, but he didn't like to see little guys, even charlatans, pushed around by big guys—not even if the big guy also happened to be his client. Nor did he see any conflict in working for both Victor and Franz at the same time. In Victor's case he was looking for a killer; in Tutin's, an arsonist—two separate things. And once he proved that Johnny Belmont was behind the attempted murder of his client, there was nothing to keep him from proving that Victor Belmont was responsible for the fire that damaged his other client's theater. Like comedy, it was all in the timing.

Seeing Johnny Belmont was not so easy. After several unanswered calls both to his apartment and his house at the lake, McGuffin dropped in one evening at the Dona Bella where Danny Biando was at his usual post. He fell on McGuffin like a desperate actor.

"What's happenin' wit' my audition?" he demanded. When McGuffin explained that there had been a fire at the theater, Danny's drooping eyelids fell and rose in gradual comprehension. "So dat means what, like a delay?"

"You're a quick read," McGuffin said.

Danny beamed at this recognition of his talent and asked McGuffin what he would have.

"A club soda and a little information," McGuffin said.

Although the bar was nearly empty, Danny leaned close and whispered, "I already tol' ya everyt'ing I know."

"Franz Tutin is renting a theater to audition a few special

138

prospects. If you'd like me to see that your name is on that list—"

"Okay, okay," he said, leaning back. He looked left and right to be sure no one was listening, then leaned forward again. "Tanya is okay. I don't know where she is, but she's okay."

"How do you know?"

"The accountant's still makin' out a check for her. I seen it."

"Where's he mailing it?"

"He ain't. Conrad Daniels picks it up."

"Daniels is delivering her checks?"

"I give you the facts, you make your own conclusions, okay?" he said, edging away from the detective.

When he returned with the club soda, McGuffin asked, "Have you seen Johnny Belmont around lately?"

"Ain't seen him in a long time, not since he heard Gregory Scott was lookin' for him."

"Do you think he's hiding out, or do you think something's happened to him?"

"Who knows?" the bartender answered. "Owin' Gregory ain't like bein' late on your Master Card."

"Where can I find Gregory?"

Danny looked over his shoulder at the clock—it was ten minutes to six—and said he should be there in a few minutes. McGuffin took his club soda and retired to a spot at the end of the bar to wait. Twenty-five minutes later Gregory Scott came in, preceded by the crossed-tie guys with Tony Pliers in the lead. Seeing McGuffin, Tony spoke softly to Gregory, who separated himself from the gang and started across the room. In marked contrast to the polyester goon squad, Gregory wore the kind of woolen pinstripe and vest that could be worn equally well by a banker or a hood.

"What brings you out on a night like this?" Gregory asked.

It was a beautiful evening. "I'm looking for Johnny Belmont."

"Why don't you ask your client where he is?"

139

"I'm afraid my client is no longer in touch with his little brother."

"That's too bad," Gregory said. He rested an elbow on the bar and remained standing, studying the detective. "I hate to see trouble between brothers. Especially when one of them is the sole support of the other. And when one of them owes me over a quarter of a million dollars, I particularly don't like to hear that his rich brother is suddenly no longer responsible for his debts. That isn't what you're trying to tell me, is it, McGuffin?"

"The name is Amos. And the only thing I'm telling you is I'm looking for Johnny Belmont. If you want to help me, fine. If you don't I'm leaving," McGuffin said, sliding off the barstool.

"Stay right where you are," Gregory commanded in a soft voice. He made no move to block him, just raised a finger in the air, and Tony Pliers bounded down the bar, quick and graceful for a big man. He stopped several paces back and waited like a well-trained police, or crook, dog for the next signal.

With his fist clenched in the pocket of his tweed jacket, McGuffin turned slightly to afford Tony a look. "If that gorilla takes one more step I'm gonna blow your brains all over the bar," he said in a voice even softer than Gregory's.

Gregory glanced uncertainly from McGuffin's concealed fist to his bare face. "Try something crazy and those guys will blow you away," he warned.

"Yeah, but you'll go first. Now tell your gorilla to get back in his cage." When Gregory hesitated, McGuffin thrust his fist forward. "Tell him."

At a second scarcely discernible signal, Tony Pliers backed away and returned to his place at the bar. McGuffin had bluffed them, but he was boxed in with nothing in his pocket but a frail fist. And even if he got out of the box and out onto the street, there was no assurance that he would be safe, for McGuffin had embarrassed Gregory Scott's spring, a robot of destruction whose only professional duty was to maim or kill his employer's debtors or enemies.

140

"I'm walking out the door," McGuffin said, sliding around Gregory. "And if you or any of your gorillas come after me, I'm gonna blow 'em away."

"I heard Californians were crazy, but I always thought it meant laid-back crazy. Or are you just stupid? You think you can come in here and tell me Johnny Belmont's disappeared and I'm just gonna tear up his IOU?" As McGuffin backed to the door, Gregory Scott followed while Tony Pliers watched intently from the bar, ready to wade through bullets if ordered. "You go back to your employer and tell him I don't give a fuck what happened to his kid brother, he still owes me and I expect it. And the next time he wants to send you out with some bullshit story about his lost brother, don't do it, because no matter how much Victor Belmont's paying you, it's not enough to get killed for."

McGuffin thanked him for the advice and continued to back toward the door. When Gregory followed him around the corner and into the foyer, McGuffin thrust his pocketed fist at him and warned him to stay back.

"I'm giving two to one that pocket's empty," the bookmaker challenged.

"Make it ten to one," McGuffin replied.

Gregory's glance went uncertainly from McGuffin's pocket to his eyes. "That's a sucker bet."

"Then wonder," McGuffin said, as he turned and pushed through the door.

Johnny Belmont surfaced two days later. A cop found him lying on the sidewalk near Roosevelt Hospital shortly after midnight, clutching a bloody handkerchief to one hand. When the handkerchief fell away as the cop pulled him to his feet, Johnny Belmont's severed little finger fell to the pavement. The cop delivered Johnny and his severed finger to the emergency room, where the finger was packed in ice and Johnny was treated for shock and loss of blood. A surgeon was called to see if the finger could be rejoined to the hand, but he decided it would be impractical.

"The finger was too badly damaged to be saved, almost as

if it had been crushed in a vice," the surgeon explained to Johnny's wife. He was very sorry but he was glad to have met Penny, as his wife watched her show all the time.

It was Penny who had phoned McGuffin and told him that her husband wanted to speak to him right away. She said she was sorry she couldn't be there when he arrived, but she had to get to the studio for a taping.

There were a few reporters at the reception desk who pounced on McGuffin the moment they heard where he was headed. Once McGuffin convinced them that he was merely a friend who knew nothing about the circumstances surrounding the accident, they were willing to reverse roles and answer McGuffin's questions. Johnny claimed he had drunkenly slammed the door on his hand while getting into a cab and the driver had rushed him to the vicinity of the nearest hospital, then driven off. McGuffin said it sounded reasonable to him and told them he knew nothing about any rumors that Johnny was in trouble with gamblers. Then he took the elevator by himself to the sixth floor where he found Johnny alone in a private room, pale and frightened, propped up in bed with a tube running from a dripping bottle to a point just above his bandaged hand.

"Do you want to tell me what happened?" McGuffin asked after expressing his sympathy. Johnny shook his head dopily. It didn't matter; McGuffin knew after Penny's description of the severed finger what had happened. "Then why did you call me?"

"I want to make a deal."

"What kind of a deal?"

"A buyout. I'll sell Victor my half of the company for forty percent of appraised value. He doesn't have to come up with all the money at once, I'll take terms. But I have to have a million dollars right now."

"A million? I thought you were in for about a quarter of a million?"

"I was desperate—all or nothing."

"And you came up with nothing."

Johnny nodded. "Make the deal, please."

142

McGuffin sat in a chair at the side of the bed, rested his elbows on his knees and studied his folded hands. He didn't like what he had to do, but Johnny Belmont, he reminded himself, had killed Angelo Tieri and, given a second chance, would kill his brother. Also Tony Pliers's mayhem, horrible though it was, was a bit of luck that could not be ignored.

"Why should Victor want to buy you out when he can force you out for nothing?" McGuffin asked.

"What do you mean?"

"I mean embezzlement, fraud, income tax evasion. Vic's got enough to put you away for a long time."

"But I didn't—"

"I know, he told you to take the money from the company."

"It's true."

"And the odd thing is, I believe you. I can see that Vic was squeezing you out, reorganizing the stock and cutting off your dividends. But you have to admit, Johnny, it wasn't entirely unfair. You weren't contributing anything to the company, or when you tried you ended up costing Vic millions of dollars."

"It was Vic who sabotoged my deals," Johnny said, struggling to rise on one elbow. "Ever since Dad died Vic's been willing to do anything to force me out."

"That might be true," McGuffin acknowledged. "Be careful, you don't want to pull your IV out," he added. "And he might have told you to take company funds just so he could charge you with embezzlement. But the fact is, Johnny, and it's unfortunate for you, he succeeded. He's got you by the short hairs, you're in no position to bargain. You've got to take what your brother's willing to offer, and that's why I'm here. You tell him what he wants to know and he'll do everything he can to see that you're treated fairly. He'll pay off Gregory Scott, he'll drop the embezzlement charges and he'll give you a fair price for your half of the company."

"He told you that?"

"He told me that and I believe him."

Johnny's short laugh resembled a cry as he flopped back

143

on the bed, giving McGuffin a start. IVs made him nervous. "You've been around him for weeks and you still don't know anything about him, do you?"

"I think I know him very well."

"Then you don't know me. I'm not stupid. I know that as soon as my brother has what he wants from me, he'll sell me out. Vic can't make a fair deal, he can only crush an opponent, even family."

"That won't happen," McGuffin promised. "You give me the information I want and I give you my word I won't do anything with it until your brother commits to a deal you can live with."

"Why should I believe you?"

"Because you have no choice. If you don't deal with me, Tony Pliers is coming back for you and this time what he pulls off might be more sorely missed than a little finger."

Johnny shuddered, then lay still. McGuffin thought he might have passed out, until he lifted his head and looked closely at him. Tears were seeping slowly from his closed eyelids. "How could he do this?" he asked. "My own brother." Then he pulled himself up and wiped his eyes with the back of his whole hand. "What do you want to know?"

McGuffin removed his notebook and pen from his jacket and asked, "What did you do with Tanya?"

"Nothing." McGuffin folded his book closed and slipped it back into his pocket. "I'm telling you the truth!" Johnny pleaded. "I told her you wanted to talk to her and she said she would and then she disappeared! I didn't have anything to do with it!"

"Then who did? Who else was involved besides Tieri? Was it Conrad Daniels?

"I don't know!"

"Or Gregory Scott?"

"I don't know!"

"What about Laird Strauss?"

"When are you gonna get it into your head, McGuffin, I don't know anything about the fucking bomb! I'll tell you what I know, but I can't tell you what I don't know!"

144

"Then you've got nothing to bargain with," McGuffin told him. "Your brother's going to go to the DA and charge you with felony embezzlement. But that might not be so bad because at least in jail you'll be safe from Tony Pliers. And by the time you get out he'll probably be dead."

"Lay off, goddammit! Haven't I been through enough already? Just tell Vic—just tell him to pay Gregory and give me a little to live on. I'll make it thirty percent. Please, you gotta help me," he begged, tears streaming from his eyes. "If you don't Tony Pliers is gonna take me apart, piece by piece." When he extended his arms in a sobbing plea, the IV pulled out and blood ran down his arm.

"You lost your needle," McGuffin said.

"Help me—" Johnny sobbed, unaware of the missing IV.

"Call me when you've got something to say," McGuffin said, then turned and walked slowly out of the room, waiting for a change of heart. None came.

He stopped at the desk to tell a nurse that Mr. Belmont had popped his IV, then continued to the elevator. In the lobby the seated press rose with military precision and accompanied him across the lobby. There was nothing new to report except that Johnny was a pillar of strength. Either that or innocent, McGuffin thought, as he pushed through the revolving door.

Chapter 17

On a Sunday evening in a partially burned out church, past and present members of the Actors Company staged a benefit performance that raised more than two hundred thousand dollars toward the restoration of the building. The quality of performance was uneven (dramatic actors singing and dancing and telling jokes to raise money?), but all the wealthy attendees (Victor Belmont and Andre Hersh were not invited) had a wonderful time. Marilyn McGuffin sang a credible "When the Lights Go on Again," with lyric changes making it appropriate to the event, while Hillary and her father (who had contributed five hundred dollars to the event—"tribute to the executioner," he had termed it) watched from the wings. Seeing so many stars in person, Hillary was only further resolved to remain in New York, while her mother, who refused to allow that the enthusiastic applause she received might have been occasioned by charity, began thinking seriously of resuming her singing career.

"You've never encouraged me in my career, Amos. I think that's the root of our problem," she complained over a bowl of chili later at Joe Allen's.

"I don't think artists should be encouraged," McGuffin growled. "All it does is prolong the agony of defeat."

"Pay no attention to your father," Marilyn advised her still-glazed-over daughter who had spotted Jeff Bridges in the brick arch. Then returning her attention to McGuffin she said, "Just because *your* career is going badly doesn't mean you should attack mine."

"Mom?" Hillary said.

"What do you mean badly? I found out that Victor Belmont's trying to take over your theater, didn't I?"

"And your divorce lawyer, don't forget that sleazeball."

"Mom, look!"

"I told you, he's no longer my sleazeball. And I know who tried to kill Victor, I just haven't been able to break him yet. You want to know what the root of our trouble is, Marilyn?" he asked, then answered. "I'm too nice a guy. If I had a little more Tony Pliers in me I wouldn't have allowed your career to interfere with our marriage. And if I'd had Tony Pliers in that hospital room with me I sure as hell would have gotten Johnny to talk. But I'm a mensch, Marilyn. I let people walk all over me, especially you."

"Yes, dear," she said, dabbing daintily with her napkin at each corner of her mouth.

"Mom, he's coming!"

"My God, it's Jeff Bridges," she said, dropping her napkin to the floor.

Jeff Bridges stopped at the table, picked up the napkin and handed it to her. "I enjoyed your song," he said, his face crinkling up in a smile that made McGuffin want to puke.

Marilyn thanked him and stared woodenly after as the star and his entourage moved to the back of the room.

"Oh, Mom!" Hillary gasped. "Can I have that napkin?"

"It's just not fair," McGuffin moaned.

The next morning McGuffin was awakened from a wonderful dream by the harsh ring of the phone. He had been back home, at Goody's Bar in San Francisco, with the cigar smoke thick as the fog outside, sitting at a long table with Hillary and Marilyn and all his friends, lawyers, politicians, even a couple of deceased clients and former adversaries, all of them eating and drinking and having a wonderful time, especially Marilyn and Hillary who agreed that this was far better than anything New York had to offer. He knew only a moment after the phone rang that it was a dream because

Goody didn't serve food, unless you counted Guinness Stout, and the biggest table in his joint could accommodate only four poker players and a dozen kibitzers, but it was a wonderful dream while it lasted.

"Hi, it's Henry," a cheery voice replied to his muffled growl.

"Who?"

"The property clerk from the sheriff's office—?"

"Oh, yeah." The long-haired crime groupie. "You're not in New York, are you?" When he said he was in his office, McGuffin yawned with relief and asked why he was phoning shortly after dawn.

"Heck, it's after eight and I told you I'd call you when I saw it, remember?"

"Not exactly."

"Don't you remember I told you I didn't see something everybody else thought they saw, but I'd call you when I saw it?" Henry asked in a puzzled voice. How could a private eye overlook so valuable a revelation?

"Okay, I remember," McGuffin assured him, lest he cry. "What did you see?"

"Nothing."

"Nothing."

"But I thought you better know, so that's why I'm calling."

"Thank you, Henry," McGuffin replied. "And if in the future you don't see anything else, please call a little later in the day, would you?"

"Sure."

"Good-bye, Henry."

"Don't you want to know what it is?"

"Who's paying for this call?"

"The county."

"Okay, tell me."

McGuffin yawned again while Henry explained that he had been over the *situs* of the crime with a comb and a magnifying glass and still had not found what he was looking for. Neither the sheriff nor anyone else would believe him, but he was convinced that it didn't exist.

148

McGuffin was about to interrupt the young crime stopper to explain that crimes were solved with existing not missing evidence, when instead he bolted up in bed and gasped, "What's missing?" Plainly exasperated by the obtuseness of everyone connected with this case, Henry spelled it out carefully. Still doubtful, McGuffin asked, "Henry, are you absolutely certain of this?"

"I'm betting my career on it, Mr. McGuffin," he answered in a firm unwavering voice.

"If you're right about this, Henry, your career is made," McGuffin assured him as he sprang from bed. He gave Henry some hurried instructions, then rang off and leapt into the shower. "Oh, what a beautiful morning," he sang, "oh, what a beautiful day," as the words of his old mentor, Miles Dwindling, rang in his ear: "Every case has its own rhythm, never force it."

Gregory Scott was not happy to hear from McGuffin.

"What the fuck you doing calling me in the middle of the night?" he shouted into the receiver.

"You want your money, don't you?" McGuffin replied.

"Yeah, I want my money. You got it?" Gregory asked, calm but wary.

"I will have if you and Tony Pliers agree to my plan."

"What plan?" Gregory asked. He listened, laughing softly from time to time while McGuffin explained the plan. "And if I do my part, Victor picks up his brother's tab?" he asked, when McGuffin had finished.

"I've already cleared it," McGuffin answered. "You give me what I want, I'll see that you get paid."

"You'd better," he said.

After working out the details and signing off, McGuffin phoned Victor. If his client refused to go along with his plan, he was going to have to watch his fingers, McGuffin realized.

"Why the hell should I pay my brother's gambling debts?" Victor protested.

"Because I said you would," McGuffin replied, as his

heart began to race. "And if you don't, Gregory will see that you lose a hell of a lot more than your pinkie."

"Okay," Victor said, after what seemed to McGuffin a long wait.

Although he was not at home and she didn't know where he could be reached, Johnny Belmont's housekeeper nevertheless took McGuffin's number, and within ten minutes he called back. McGuffin inquired about his finger, was told it was healing satisfactorily, then informed Johnny that he had spoken to Victor and he was willing to entertain a buyout.

"How much?" Johnny demanded.

"I don't think it's the sort of thing we can do over the phone," McGuffin replied.

"Just tell me the parameters. What are we talking about, forty percent—thirty percent?"

"I'm sure that under the circumstances you'll find your brother to be very generous."

"Yeah, right. What about up-front money? I gotta have at least a million right away."

"Your debt with Gregory Scott will be taken care of once we've settled on the terms of the buyout," McGuffin responded in the calm voice of a man bargaining from strength.

"Not just my debt, I gotta have a little extra," Johnny pleaded. "I got expenses."

"Your brother is aware of that," McGuffin assured him. "I've arranged for the three of us to have dinner tonight at my hotel, the Gramercy Park."

"Tonight?"

"Victor is anxious to have this done with as soon as possible. And I assumed you'd feel the same way."

"Okay, I'll meet with him," Johnny agreed.

"Eight o'clock," McGuffin said.

McGuffin waited in the lobby, trying not to worry, telling himself that he hadn't made a foolish mistake, that they would bring it off without a hitch. Until only a short while ago it had seemed an elegantly simple plan that would put an end to his troubles, but now, sitting in a chair opposite the hotel entrance while Tony Pliers stood hidden beside the door, he realized it could be the beginning of more trouble than he had ever had in his life. He would be an accessory to a felony, for God's sake! And how could he have thought that a frustrated preppie and a boneheaded bonecrusher could pull it off? Maybe Johnny wouldn't show. It was already eight-fifteen and Tony was getting fidgety, glancing from his watch to McGuffin with a shrug. Look at the dummy, we're not supposed to know each other and he's making faces at me. I'll go to prison, lose my license, my daughter— Why did I ever leave San Francisco?

Oh, shit! It was Johnny Belmont stepping out of a limousine. He looked up and down the street, then leaned over and spoke to the driver through the open window, and a moment later the car pulled away, leaving Johnny alone on the sidewalk. He tugged at the lapels of his jacket, then started for the glass door as McGuffin jumped to his feet and Tony, only a fraction of a second later, pushed through the same glass door, freezing Johnny on the sidewalk. Tony was there, reaching for him, it was going to work, when suddenly something appeared between them, a small crouched person, followed by a collision and a flying skateboard. The boy hurtled like a rag doll and fell to the pavement while Tony hopped about on one foot, clutching at his shin, and one by one a group of skateboarders, like urban surfers, glided to a stop on the paved beach. One pulled his fallen comrade to his feet, while the others surrounded Tony and a chorus of angry voices turned heads in the lobby.

The whole thing lasted only several seconds, barely enough time for McGuffin to get through the door as Johnny bolted. Tony Pliers roared like a bear with a hot foot as he pushed through the kids and hobbled after the fleeing playboy, followed by McGuffin, who quickly overtook Tony but remained a poor second to Johnny Belmont, with the gang on skateboards temporarily bringing up the rear. The skateboard kids screamed like banshees, and the crowd on the street, quickly aware that something was happening, joined

151

in the shouting for no discernible reason. Johnny was pulling away, McGuffin was no match for him, until a black sedan squealed suddenly around the corner in front of him and Johnny ran into the side of the car and came directly back, spilling to the pavement in a dead fall, where he lay motionless long enough for McGuffin to get to him. McGuffin pinned him to the ground and looked back to Tony for help, just as he saw the first skateboarder fall on him, followed by another and another, clamping on Tony's arms and legs and back while he thrashed and roared like King Kong until a skateboard across the shins sent him to the pavement under their flailing weight.

Now Johnny began to moan and stir. A curious crowd was moving forward and McGuffin was about to bolt and run when a pair of black-and-white saddle shoes came into view and he realized Gregory Scott was driving the car Johnny had bounced off. They quickly pulled Johnny to his feet and pushed him through the dented door, then Gregory jumped behind the wheel and they were off, McGuffin struggling to hold the revived Johnny in the car.

"Pop him, pop him!" Gregory shouted, as he skidded the car around a corner.

After some wrestling for position, McGuffin gave him a short but efficient jab to the point of the chin and Johnny Belmont went out for the second time. "Where the hell are we going?" McGuffin shouted, as Gregory careened around a second corner and sped down a narrow street.

"Back around the block to get Tony!" he shouted back.

"No! The crowd—the cops will be there!" McGuffin protested.

"Get ready to pull him in."

Gregory rounded the corner and, with a hand on the horn, headed the car into the crowd assembled on the street to watch a man being taunted by a bunch of kids with skateboards. When the car jerked to a halt McGuffin opened the door and shouted to Tony, who was hit across the back with a skateboard when he looked away. "Get in, get in!"

"Help him!" Gregory ordered.

"Fuck you!" McGuffin shouted, as Tony thrashed through the enraged kids and stumbled breathlessly into the back of the car. McGuffin reached across him and pulled the door closed as Gregory leaned on the horn and the gas pedal and the car screeched away.

"Fuckin' little motherfuckers, put 'em all in a fuckin' jail!" Tony moaned, while rubbing at his battered places. "Look! Look what the little fuckers did!"

"Shut up, I'm trying to drive!" Gregory called as he sped down Broadway, weaving between cars.

"Pull over!" McGuffin shouted. "I'm calling it off!"

"Like hell you are!"

"Hey, where'd you get him?" Tony asked, seeing Johnny Belmont for the first time, crumpled in the corner.

"We ran into him," McGuffin said. "Listen to me, Gregory, they've got a make on the car. Put Johnny and me out and get rid of it. The plan is finished, we'll never get to Brooklyn in a hot car."

"Don't be stupid, half the cars in Brooklyn are hot."

"You won't get through the tunnel."

"We're not going through the tunnel."

When Johnny began to stir, Tony leaned his face in close so Johnny could see who it was, then told him to be quiet and not move, which had the desired effect. Johnny went rigid and mute with fear, and McGuffin worried that he might have a heart attack before he was able to get what he wanted from him. When they passed a police car near Canal Street without incident, McGuffin began to hope they might make it, and when they started up and over the Brooklyn Bridge, he sat back quietly in the seat.

"What are you gonna do to me?" Johnny asked, when they had crossed the bridge into Brooklyn.

"I wish I knew," McGuffin said, staring out the window, a tourist in Brooklyn. They wound under the bridge among dilapidated buildings surrounded by high fences topped by coiled razor ribbon shining dully in hazy cones of light. It was a place charged with the din of grinding gears and whining conveyors and pounding steel during the day, but at night nothing moved but silent rats.

153

They stopped before one of these fences and Gregory got out to open the padlocked gate, then got back in and drove around to the back of the building where the lighted spires of Manhattan hove into view across the river. He parked beside a steel door with one bare bulb burning above it, got out and opened Johnny's door. He ordered him out, but Johnny didn't move, so McGuffin pushed and Gregory pulled and they got him outside. Tony held him by the collar while Gregory opened the locked door, went inside and switched the lights on. It was a dump stacked with baled paper and cardboard and the floor was covered with scraps, which made walking difficult for Tony, who had the added weight of Johnny on his hands. They slipped and slid across the floor to a small enclosed office where Tony dropped Johnny on a short stool and began tying his hands in front of him while McGuffin looked away from Johnny's frightened face, out the single dirty window in the tiny space. They were on a canal or inlet, black and still as pooled oil, and on the opposite bank lay several burned-out automobile hulks, one partly submerged.

"Please don't hurt me," Johnny begged. "I'll get the money. Tell them, McGuffin."

His thin voice bounced off the glass and back into McGuffin's face with the sour smell of fear. McGuffin stuck his hands in his pockets and hunched his shoulders at the sound of a slap, followed by Johnny's sobs.

"It's too late for the money," Gregory said. "You embarrassed me with my clients and I gotta clear that up. I can't leave my clients with the impression that somebody can run a tab and then laugh at me."

"Laugh! You cut off my finger, for God's sake! Who's laughing? Please, Gregory, don't do it! You know me, you know my brother—you know you'll get your money! I'll pay double!"

"Johnny, you have to understand, there's only one thing you can give me that'll restore my image and that's not money," Gregory explained patiently. "You ever been to the Caribbean, Johnny? Because that's where you're going,

154

inside one of these bales. Only your hands and your head won't be going with you. Or is that the other way around? But don't worry because we'll put them in a lead box and give them a nice burial at sea—if you can call that slime pit out there the sea." Tony's laugh sounded like boulders in an oil drum. "Keep an eye on him while Tony and I get the saw," he said.

McGuffin said he would and they went out, slamming the door behind them. He continued to stare out the window, accompanied by Johnny's groans and the rhythmic squeaking of the rocking stool. "I'm sorry it has to be this way, Johnny."

"You fucker—no good motherfucker—" he bawled. "How much did he pay you to sell me out?"

"No, Johnny, you got it wrong. I didn't sell you out for money, I did it out of pride," McGuffin replied in a righteous voice as he turned to the prisoner. "And it's important to me that you understand that before they—well, it's important to me, that's all. You see, Johnny, I don't like to leave a case unresolved, especially when I know who the perpetrator is but can't prove it. When that happens I get terribly frustrated, my pride is wounded, so I have to take extralegal measures to see that the guilty are punished."

"You can't do that, you can't be my judge, jury and executioner!" he wailed.

"I have to," McGuffin answered, with a helpless shrug. "As things stood you'd never have been tried."

"If I confess will you get me out of this?"

"I'd much rather see you go to prison than the Caribbean, if only for my reputation," McGuffin answered. "You tell me everything I want to know and I'll take you out of here."

"But what about them?" he asked, with a nod at the door.

"Don't worry, I'll get you out of here even if I have to kill them," McGuffin said, taking a gun from his jacket pocket. It was, the clerk at the gift shop had assured him, an exact replica of a World War II Luger.

155

"Okay, I tried to kill my brother, cut me loose," he blurted.

"Not so fast."

"They'll be back, for Christ's sake!"

At that moment the door opened and Gregory entered, followed by Tony with a rusty saw in one hand. "Okay, we got the saw," Gregory said, then stopped when he saw the gun in McGuffin's hand. "What the fuck's going on?"

"Change of plans," McGuffin said. "Up against the wall."

Protesting, Gregory and his spring took their positions against the wall while McGuffin carefully removed a small automatic from each of them and dropped both the guns into his jacket pocket. "Okay, Johnny, you were saying—?"

"I said I did it, what the fuck else you want to know?"

"Who helped you?"

"Angelo Tieri, you already know that."

"Who else, who introduced you to Angelo?"

"Tanya."

"And who introduced you to Tanya? Was it Conrad Daniels?"

"Yeah."

"Where is Tanya now?"

"I have no idea and that's the truth."

McGuffin believed him. "Where's Daniels's hunting lodge?"

"His lodge? It's up in the Adirondacks, northwest of Saratoga Springs. You want to know exactly?" McGuffin said he did and Johnny told him exactly how to get there.

"Who else was involved with the bombing?"

"Nobody else."

"You want to go to the Caribbean?" McGuffin asked.

"For Christ's sake, you think I'd try to protect somebody at a time like this? I'm telling you the truth, it was just Tanya, Angelo and me! I was having an affair with Tanya and I told her how my brother was trying to screw me out of the company. Then she told me she knew a guy who would take care of my brother. I said whattaya mean 'take care' and she said kill him and I said forget it, but she kept after me about it all the time and—"

156

"Save the clemency plea for the judge, just give me the facts," McGuffin ordered.

"Okay, okay. So I finally said I'd do it and she introduced me to Angelo and he said he'd do it for fifty thousand and I said okay, he'd get it when I got my money, after the job was done."

"And he agreed?"

"Not at first, but Tanya assured him I was good for it and he said okay."

"Who suggested a bomb?"

"Angelo. I thought he was gonna shoot him, but Angelo preferred a bomb. He said it was more traditional."

"Where did he get it?"

"How do I know? He told me he could get a bomb, that was all I cared about."

"What kind of bomb?"

"I don't know what the fuck kind of bomb it was. I didn't even see it except for the briefcase he was carrying it in. He said that when Vic started the car it would go off and I said fine, that's what I want."

"Okay, tell me about the night it did go off. Was Tanya with you?"

"Not exactly. She and Angelo followed me up to the house in his car, in case he got lost. We stopped at the head of the driveway and I told him how to walk up to the garage without being seen, then I drove up to the house."

"Alone."

"Yeah. You were right—I lied about sneaking Tanya into the house, that was dumb. She stayed in the car and waited while Angelo went to plant the bomb, then the two of them were supposed to drive back to New York."

"Why didn't just she and Angelo drive up together, plant the bomb and go back to New York? Why did you want to be at the scene of the crime when the explosion occurred?"

"I didn't, that was Angelo's idea. I took him as far as the garage and showed him which car to wire, then I waited in the driveway. Only I should have waited a lot farther away. Then when Tanya heard the explosion she split. And that's the truth, the whole truth and nothing but the truth."

"It might be the truth, but it's not the whole truth," McGuffin said, as he dug the two small automatics out of his coat pocket. "Think fast," he said, and tossed them over Johnny's head.

Johnny watched incredulously as Gregory and Tony snatched them out of the air. "What the fuck are you doing?" he shouted.

"April fool," Gregory said.

"Hold this," McGuffin said, pushing the Luger in Johnny's bound hands.

Johnny took the gun, hefted it and pronounced it "A fake."

"The whole thing was a fake," McGuffin said, untying Johnny's hands. "Victor doesn't want to buy you out, he wants to drive you out without anything. But don't worry, I promised Gregory he'd take care of your debt in exchange for helping me get your confession."

"Sons a bitches," Johnny said, as McGuffin took his toy gun back.

Sitting in the backseat with Johnny during the ride back to Manhattan, Tony Pliers looked at him several times and laughed. He couldn't help it, it was the funniest thing that had happened since the night he pulled Johnny's finger off.

Chapter 18

McGuffin pulled off the New York Thruway at Saratoga Springs and drove slowly down the main street, past grand old hotels and Victorian mansions, spilling over with the wealthy horsey set just a few months before, now dark and empty. Half an hour later the sun rose behind him, covering the rolling hills with a gray light that exploded finally in gold over the Great Sacandaga Lake. A short while after that he saw the snow-covered peaks in the distance that marked the valley where the lodge would be, where Tanya did or did not temporarily reside.

He found Snake Road and turned north as Johnny had instructed, across the covered bridge and past the watermill to the timber gate that marked the entrance to Conrad Daniels's hunting lodge. After about half a mile he glimpsed a stone chimney sticking up through the clearing and quickly slowed the car to a crawl. At a break in the wall of trees he eased the car off the road and into a copse of evergreens, switched off the ignition, stepped out of the car and quietly closed the door.

He pulled the collar of his tweed jacket up, clutched the lapels closed and started up the drive. The early-morning mountain air was a startling change from autumn in New York. After a couple of hundred yards the road swung lazily to the left, revealing the lodge in a clearing at the foot of a snowcapped peak. It was an enormous log building with a broad porch running across the front, gables sprouting from the shake roof and balconies jutting out from the upper rooms.

Staying within the trees, he made his way to the edge of the graveled parking area where a dark-blue mud-splattered Cadillac rested rakishly in front of the stairs, a lonely forlorn thing, hopelessly out of its element. There were no other vehicles in evidence and no noise or other sign of activity coming from the lodge. A single window above and to one side of the front entrance was open several inches, releasing a white lace curtain that fluttered listlessly in the breeze. He took a deep breath and dashed across the parking lot, then up the stairs and across the wide porch to the massive front door. It was made of smooth half logs and hung with thick iron hinges, but the lock was a piece of cake. He stepped inside, pulled the door closed after him and waited. A set of stairs directly ahead led to a second-floor balcony with a hallway spoking off either side. Downstairs to the right was a set of glass doors opening to an enormous dining room, and on the log walls everywhere, scores of trophies, elk, moose, deer, bears, boar, as well as African lions and tigers and a great tusked elephant above the cavernous fireplace. To the left was the library with a pair of billiard tables, along with the ubiquitous stuffed game birds, a sly fox and, of all things, one particularly revered Irish Setter.

A veritable charnel house, McGuffin said to himself as he removed the toy gun from his jacket and started across the foyer to the carpeted stairs. He edged past the stuffed bear at the top of the stairs and moved along the balcony to the hallway. The bedroom with the fluttering curtain should be behind the first door, he guessed, as he gently tried the door.

The knob turned and the door opened with a faint squeak that caused a slight stir under the thick comforter heaped over the canopied timberpost bed. He could see only long black hair until he pulled the blankets away and clamped a hand on a bare shoulder.

"Tanya!"

160

"Wha—!" she exclaimed, bolting up and out from under her modest cover. There could be no mistaking those breasts, it was Tanya.

"Take it easy. I'm not going to hurt you," McGuffin assured her in a quiet soothing voice.

"Who—who—?" she tried, staring at the toy gun.

"My name is Amos McGuffin," he answered. "I just want to ask you some questions."

"The detective—"

"That's right."

"I don't know nothing, honest," she said, her dark sleepy eyes widening quickly.

"Then why did you run up here and hide on me?"

"I'm not hiding," she said, which was certainly true for the moment. "I'm on vacation."

"Are you alone?"

"Yes. I mean no," she quickly corrected, but too late. McGuffin slipped the toy gun back into his pocket, as she improvised a protector lurking somewhere in the building. "Can I get dressed?" she asked, suddenly tiring of her own story.

"After you've answered my questions," McGuffin replied. "You were with Johnny Belmont on the night of the explosion."

"Is that a question?"

"Johnny told me all about it—or at least as much as he knows. Now I want to hear it from you."

Tanya continued to insist that she knew nothing while McGuffin insisted calmly that she did. He recited everything Johnny had told him about that fatal night, mentioning the details that only she, Johnny and Angelo Tieri could know. Finally she slumped forward and stared vacantly out the window where the white curtain fluttered. "Why'd Johnny talk?" she asked in a weak voice.

"To save himself," McGuffin answered. "And I'm going to give you the same chance, if you'll tell me who's behind this. You help me now and I'll help you later with the district attorney."

"Yeah, I bet you will," she said, brushing the hair from her face.

"Face it, you've got no choice. Johnny's testimony by itself is enough to put you away for a long time, unless you start cooperating with me right now."

"Fuck you, you're no cop. I don't have to say nothing to you."

"Fine, we'll talk to the DA," McGuffin said, reaching for her.

"Wait!" she cried, pulling away. McGuffin waited while she ran her fingers through her hair and got comfortable. "How do I know you'll be straight with me?"

"I'm working for Victor Belmont. He doesn't want you and he doesn't want his little brother, he just wants the man who's behind the attempt on his life. And we both know who that is."

"Do we?" she asked.

McGuffin nodded and looked around the room. "Your host."

"Conrad? Did Johnny tell you it was Conrad?"

"You know he didn't because Johnny doesn't know Conrad's involved. But you do," he added, and waited to see if he was right. He was, he could see it in her face.

She nodded slowly before replying, "Yeah, it was Conrad. He told me not to worry, nothing was gonna happen. What a lotta shit."

"It was Conrad who introduced you to Johnny?" She nodded. "Why?"

"He wanted me to get close to him, pretend to be in love with him, get him to tell me things."

"But you weren't in love with him, you were in love with Angelo Tieri."

"Yeah, I was in love with Angelo," she said. "And Angelo was in love with me, so I told Conrad I couldn't sleep with no other guy. But then Angelo told me I should, I should go to bed with Johnny Belmont and he wouldn't mind. Wouldn't mind! I know I shouldn't a done it, but I was so fucking strung out on the guy I didn't know what was what, so I let him talk me into it," she said, dabbing at her eyes with the sheet.

"And after you started sleeping with him, what did you find out about Johnny?"

"I found out he was a fucking crybaby, that's what I found out," she said, pulling the sheet away from her now-dry eyes and letting it fall to her lap. She reached across the bed for her cigarettes, proffered one to McGuffin who shook his head, then lighted it. She blew smoke into the room and settled back against the timber headboard with a sigh. "He said his brother was always on his case, wouldn't give him enough money, wouldn't let him have his say in the company, shit like that. I told Conrad, the guy is a fucking whiner, what do you want from me, but Connie tells me to stay with him. And when I really get fed up, Angelo goes to work on me, telling me Conrad's our horse, he's gonna fix it so we can get married. So naturally I go along with it even though I don't see the point."

She took a deep drag, held it down for a long time, then exhaled sibilantly. "Until I tell Conrad that Johnny wants to kill his brother. Like it was just talk, he don't have the balls, but Conrad gloms on to it like it's real news. He tells me to tell Johnny that I can get him a hitter. I says whattaya, Conrad, fucking crazy? But he says tell him, so I tell him." She took a quick toke then fixed McGuffin with a sad look. "I guess that's the part I shouldn't a done, but by then it was too late. You just don't tell Conrad you aren't gonna do something."

"I think you got it backward," McGuffin corrected. "I think it was Conrad's idea to kill Victor and it was your job to sell Johnny on the plan."

"I had nothing to do with it!"

"Tanya, if I'm going to help you I have to know everything exactly as it happened. Because if any part of your story doesn't check out, if the DA thinks you're an unreliable witness, he'll cut a deal with Conrad or Johnny and let you swing. Understand?"

She nodded slowly. "Yeah, I understand."

163

"Good. So Conrad told you to persuade Johnny to kill his brother." She nodded again. "And you told Johnny you knew a hitter and Johnny said to get him."

"Yeah, like that. I really didn't think he'd go for it, but as long as somebody else was gonna do the dirty work, Johnny could hack it. So I told Conrad—okay, he wants to meet the hit man, who is he? And Conrad says Angelo. Angelo! I thought it was Tony Pliers or somebody like that. What's Angelo know about that shit? I tried to talk him out of it, but Angelo said he wasn't really gonna kill nobody, he was just gonna put a bomb on a car. I says whatta you know about bombs and he says Conrad's gonna show him. Jesus, I gotta piss."

"Go ahead, but leave the door open," McGuffin directed.

Muttering, Tanya bounded out of bed and into the bathroom.

"So I arrange for Johnny and Angelo to meet," she went on over the sounds of urination. "And Angelo lays it all out and Johnny says it sounds neat, for Christ's sake. So everybody agrees, Angelo and I are gonna follow Johnny up to the house and Angelo's gonna plant the bomb, then him and me'll drive back. Only that ain't the way it happened," she said, followed by the flushing toilet.

"Why did you and Johnny go along?" McGuffin called over the falling water.

"That was Angelo's idea," she called back. "Johnny didn't want any part of it, but Angelo said he wouldn't do it unless Johnny went with him as far as the garage. That way Angelo was sure it was safe."

"Did Angelo want him to go inside the garage with him when he planted the bomb?" he called, as she opened a faucet.

"Yeah, but I guess he didn't," she called back.

"Apparently," McGuffin replied in a voice that couldn't be heard over the rushing water.

A moment later she stepped back into the room and asked, "Can I get dressed?"

164

"Go ahead," McGuffin said. When she moved to the dresser he leapt to her side.

"It's just my underwear," she said, opening the drawer for him.

It was nearly empty. "It doesn't look as if you were planning to stay long," he observed.

"I wasn't," she answered, stepping into her bikini bottoms. "Conrad said it would just be until you got tired of nosing around. How'd you find out I was here?"

"A wild guess," McGuffin said, picking up the sweater that lay over the back of the chair. It was cashmere with a V neck. Tanya took it from him and pulled it over her head. The tight jeans, which were followed by a pair of white boots, did not go on so effortlessly. McGuffin stood in the doorway while she washed and brushed her teeth, then sat on the bed and waited while she combed her long hair. There was more to tell her, but this wasn't the time.

When she was finished she got to her feet and turned to him. "What happens to me now?"

"We go back to New York," McGuffin answered. In fact, he would deliver her to the sheriff and continue on to New York alone, but there was no need to tell her this just yet.

"Will I have to go to jail?"

"You're an important witness. You'll be treated very well and you'll be protected," McGuffin answered.

"Witness," she repeated, savoring it. "That's right, I didn't kill nobody. Angelo's death was an accident."

"It wasn't an accident," he said.

"What do you mean?"

"Get your coat."

"I want to know what you mean," she said, as she followed him down the stairs.

"In due time," McGuffin said. He did not want a distraught passenger all the way to the sheriff's office. He helped her with her fur coat then led her outside, down the porch stairs and past the muddy Cadillac.

"Hey, where's your car?" she said, stopping and looking around.

"Down the road."

"Shit," she muttered, picking her way over the stones after him.

They were standing in the middle of the parking lot when McGuffin heard the car and reached into his pocket for the toy Luger. A moment later a black Mercedes cleared the trees and made directly for them before veering off and sliding to a halt. Both front doors opened and Conrad Daniels stepped out from behind the wheel with an automatic resting lazily in his hand.

"What are you going to do, McGuffin, shoot me with a toy gun?" he called.

McGuffin let the gun fall to the ground as Victor Belmont climbed out of the car. "I had an idea Tony would talk."

"That's what I pay him for," Conrad answered.

"Did you also pay him to kill Nina Tieri?" McGuffin asked.

"I told you he was gonna be trouble," Conrad reminded Victor.

"Lay off," Victor said. He was unshaven and his eyes were red from lack of sleep or worry.

"I didn't tell him nothin'," Tanya said, moving gingerly toward Conrad.

"It doesn't matter," Conrad assured her, then motioned with the gun and ordered them inside.

Uncertain of her status, Tanya walked directly behind McGuffin, followed by Victor and Conrad. Once inside the foyer, Conrad ordered them to stop. "You go upstairs and wait in your room until I call you," he said, motioning Tanya to the stairs. "You in the dining room," he added, prodding McGuffin with the gun.

She moved slowly up the stairs and along the balcony, watching until McGuffin was seated facing the door. Conrad and Victor took seats at the opposite side of the dining table, Victor still in his coat and hat, as if he expected to leave soon. Conrad placed the automatic on the table and leaned back in his chair, as if he were in no hurry to go

166

anywhere, perhaps only waiting for McGuffin to go for the gun.

"What did she tell you?" Conrad asked.

"As much as she knows," McGuffin answered. "That you installed her with Johnny and enticed him into blowing up Victor."

"He didn't need much enticing," Victor put in.

"I'm sure," McGuffin agreed. "The kid is worthless, you had good reason to try to drive him out of the company. You reorganized the stock and stopped his dividends, you cut his salary and you set him up for embezzlement and tax fraud, but he still wouldn't go. So you decided to kill him. And that's when you went to Conrad. Have I got it right so far?"

"Right as rain," Conrad answered. "When Vic came to me and told me he wanted to kill his little brother, I was shocked, as you can well imagine. Until I found out from Vic what a little ratfucker he was. Then I had to agree with my friend here, Johnny Belmont was serving no purpose on this earth. He was not only a great financial burden to his brother, who had always treated him like a son, but his affairs with other women were a constant source of pain and humiliation to his lovely wife, who also happens to be a TV celebrity," he added.

"And she has great legs," McGuffin remarked.

"That too. But to make a long story short, I decided to assist my old friend in what I now considered a most deserving and humane enterprise."

"For which he charged me four hundred thousand," Victor added.

"Two hundred," Conrad corrected.

"Let me tell it," Victor said, removing his hat and placing it on the table near McGuffin. He leaned forward on his elbows and pointed a finger at Conrad. "He wanted to hire some torpedo to just gun Johnny down, until I pointed out that I'd be the most likely suspect. Never mind that the cops couldn't prove anything, I've got a reputation to uphold—I

167

didn't want to end up like Claus von Bulow. So I specified that it had to be a bomb."

"And I agreed, two hundred to blow his little brother off the face of the earth. A fair price, don't you think?"

Before McGuffin could answer, Victor was talking about Angelo Tieri. "He told me he had just the man for the job, an ex-ballplayer with a lovely wife and kids, who was like a son to him. I said, Conrad, wait, you don't understand—It's got to look like Johnny was trying to kill me. Johnny and the bomber have to blow up together. So you know what he said?" Victor asked, smiling, pointing at Conrad.

"What did he say?"

"He said, 'No problem, it'll just cost you another two hundred thousand.' I said, 'You're going to charge me the same price for the bomber as you are for my brother? Don't I at least get a quantity discount?' And he said, 'Vic, what can I tell you, Angelo's like a son to me.' "

McGuffin waited silently while both men laughed at this story. It was the kind of story they would tell again and again until finally the bare punch line, 'He's like a son to me,' would send them into paroxysms of laughter that no one around them would understand. He hoped they would have the opportunity to tell it to each other in jail over and over again, but at the moment that prospect seemed far less likely than his own imminent demise.

"Unfortunately Johnny refused at the last minute to go into the garage with Angelo like he was supposed to," Victor added in a suddenly somber voice.

"So that's when you got this idea to hire an investigator, somebody to discover Johnny's embezzlement and his connection to Angelo while you made a great show of protecting his innocence all the way to prison. Only of course Johnny didn't steal a dime from the company, you set him up. That was to have been his motive for attempting to kill you, which you would have regretfully announced after he had blown himself up."

"Actually I hadn't intended to hire a detective," Victor corrected. "When my plan backfired I was prepared to call it quits. Conrad was afraid that a sharp detective might somehow connect him to the plot. But when I met you, McGuffin, a drunken detective from out of town, it was as if God had sent you to me."

"I was not at my best that night," McGuffin admitted.

"I knew the night you came to my apartment that you weren't as dumb as Victor said," Conrad complained. "But it was too late, there was nothing I could do about it."

"Except kill Nina Tieri," McGuffin said.

"That was her fault, not mine. She was told not to talk to anybody, but she did, so I had to send Tony Pliers around."

"It must have caused you a lot of pain."

"Shut up, McGuffin. Or aren't you in enough trouble already?" Daniels asked.

"Me? Sheriff Strock knows you guys blew up Angelo and attempted to kill Johnny and you tell me *I'm* in trouble?"

"Strock? He knows about this?" Victor demanded.

"Relax, Victor, the cops know nothing. It's the last ploy of the desperate detective, right, McGuffin?"

"If I'm bluffing, how did I learn that the bomb you provided Angelo was sabotaged?"

"A wild guess," Conrad answered easily. "Nobody ever said you were incompetent—except for Victor, and I think he's changed his mind."

"I might be competent, but I don't know how to put a detonated bomb back together piece by piece," McGuffin replied. "But the sheriff has a bomb expert who did just that and do you know what he found? Or let me correct that, do you know what he didn't find?" McGuffin waited, he had their attention.

"He didn't find any evidence of a switch." His eyes fastened for a moment on Conrad's inexpressive face then panned to Victor's confused expression. "That means the bomb was not designed to explode when the ignition was turned on, but when the wires were attached to the car. But of course you knew that," he said with a nod to Conrad. "Unfortunately for Angelo, he didn't. He just assumed that under all that electrical tape there was a switch. After all, the man who gave him the bomb was like a father to him."

"They know!" Victor exclaimed. "He's not just guessing."

Again Conrad told him to relax. His voice was calm, but his eyes danced. "If he spoke to the cops, why aren't they here? Why'd they let him come up here alone?" he argued.

"I told the sheriff I could handle this myself, that I'd swing by and see if Tanya was here. If I'd known Tony was on your payroll I wouldn't have come alone."

"That's bullshit! If they wanted her there'd be a dozen cars in the parking lot right now."

"The sheriff's no longer in any hurry," McGuffin said. "Not after I told him Johnny's taped confession was in the mail."

"What confession?"

"Tony didn't tell you about the confession? I got Johnny on tape, witnessed by Gregory Scott and Tony Pliers."

"Oh, God—" Victor moaned. "We're fucked."

"We're not fucked. Shut up and let me think. The only people Johnny can implicate are Angelo and Tanya. He didn't know anything about our part in it. And the only person Tanya can implicate is me. Therefore, all we have to do is get rid of Tanya and we're clear. And McGuffin, of course," Conrad added.

"You're off the rails!" Victor shouted. "If you kill him and Tanya, we're the first people they'll come after."

"They can come as often as they want, but they'll never be able to prove a thing. Trust me, Vic."

"Sure, trust him, he's done great so far. Listen to me, Victor, because if you don't you're dead meat."

"Shut the fuck up, McGuffin, or—!" Conrad began, then stopped.

It was the involuntary look of surprise on McGuffin's face that stopped Victor. When he turned around to see what McGuffin was looking at, he gasped her name and reached back for the gun on the table, but McGuffin had recovered a split second sooner. He too reached for the gun, barely beating Conrad to it, but failed to snatch it cleanly from the

170

tabletop. Instead he slapped it to the floor and lunged after it as the room was rocked by a loud explosion and shattering glass and Tanya's scream, "Don't move!"

Conrad stood stock still as Tanya advanced on him with an ancient double-barrel shotgun, one barrel curling blue smoke. McGuffin lay on the floor, his hand only a few feet from the automatic just on the other side of a dining chair. Victor too was on his feet, frozen beside Conrad. McGuffin expected to see a gaping hole in one of them, but he saw only a trickle of blood falling from Conrad's hand where he had been hit by a random pellet or two. The only other hole was in the window some three or four feet to the lawyer's right. Tanya was either not a marksperson, or that first shot was a very accurate warning.

"There's still one more shell in here and I know what to do with it," she said.

"Tanya, be careful," Conrad pleaded.

"You mean like you were careful with Angelo?" she asked. "Angelo who was like a son to you? You prick. How could you?"

"I don't know what you heard, Tanya, but—"

"I heard it all," she said, still walking, gun at the ready. "How you sent Angelo off to kill himself. How you were gonna kill me."

"Tanya, believe me, it never would have come to that. I just wanted McGuffin to—"

"You knew—we were gonna be married," she said.

"Tanya, put the gun down and we'll talk," Conrad urged.

"Move another inch and I'll blow your balls off," she said, thrusting the gun in that vicinity, backing him over the table. She was only a few yards away, close enough that she couldn't miss, but also close enough that Conrad or Victor might make a successful lunge for the gun.

"I'd never do anything to hurt you," Conrad assured her. "Angelo wasn't going to marry you, he was only using you."

"That's a lie."

"Ask yourself, would he, an Italian Catholic, have told you to sleep with Johnny if he was in love with you, if he

171

had intended to divorce his wife and marry you? You know he wouldn't and so do I, because he told me. That's when I decided to take Angelo out with Johnny—because he deserved it. I could have sent Tony or somebody else to do the job, but when I saw him fuck you over like that, I was pissed. I think too much of you to allow anybody to do that to you, and that's when I decided Angelo had to be the guy."

"You think a lot of me, do you?"

"Yes, Tanya, I do."

"Is that why you let all your friends fuck me? Johnny and Laird Strauss and all—"

"That was business," Conrad pleaded. "I had to place Angelo with Strauss and I was forced to use you as an inducement. I wouldn't have used you if it could have been avoided, Tanya, you know that."

"Ask him why it couldn't be avoided," McGuffin called from under the table.

"Shut up!" Conrad ordered.

"Answer him," Tanya demanded.

"It was a chance to kill two birds with one stone. Connect Strauss to Angelo and create the impression that he and Johnny were working together to kill Victor and take over Manhattan."

"Rather flimsy evidence for a conviction," McGuffin opined from the floor.

"We weren't looking for a conviction, just rumor and innuendo—enough to ruin Laird's chances of ever getting another project off the ground. Johnny was Victor's idea, Laird was mine," he added.

"What about all the others?" she demanded. "What about the congressman and the guys from the mayor's office and your union buddies, and the guy who cuts your hair and shines you shoes? What about all them, was that business?"

"Tanya, I've made some mistakes, I don't deny that. But not about Angelo, and that's what we're talking about here. Even while he was going with you he was fucking other

172

women, right here in this place. I saw it, I know. He had no respect for you, he had no feeling at all for you."

"No!" she screamed, as at the same moment Conrad saw his chance and took it.

At the sound of the gun McGuffin scrambled after the automatic, snatched it up and rolled clear of the table, then came up in a genuflect, gun pointed to where Conrad had stood a moment before. It took him a moment to find his quarry in the gunsight, seated on the floor beside the shattered window, but it didn't matter. Putting a bullet through Conrad Daniels now would be like shooting through a tunnel.

When McGuffin took the warm shotgun from her, she collapsed against him and sobbed, while Victor stared transfixed at the lifeless body against the blood-splattered wall. McGuffin waited until she stopped crying, then peeled her off and sat her down on a chair. Victor looked down at her as if she had fallen from the sky. "Where'd you get this?" McGuffin asked, laying the shotgun across the end of the table.

"Out of the gun case, in the billiard room," she answered. "Conrad left it for me 'cuz I was alone up here. I guess he forgot."

"I guess he did."

It took Victor only a moment more to regain his composure. "I want to make a deal," he said.

"What kind of a deal?"

"All you have to do is let me go and I'll give you a hundred thousand dollars."

"What kind of a guy do you think I am?" McGuffin asked. "I have to have at least a million."

"A million—!"

"Maybe more."

"Okay, a million."

McGuffin whistled appreciatively. "But what about him?" he asked, pointing the automatic at the bloody corpse.

"We'll bury him in the woods. Nobody will ever find him."

McGuffin placed the barrel of the gun against his cheek

and nodded thoughtfully. "What about Tanya? Are you going to pay her a million to keep quiet?"

"Of course not," he replied, appalled at the suggestion. Tanya had shot her wad, McGuffin still held his gun.

"But you've got to pay her something or she's going to talk. And if you don't pay her what you pay me, she's going to be resentful, and you know what that means."

"Of course. We'll kill her too."

"We—"

Victor shook his head, impatient at such squeamishness. "Give me the gun, I'll do it."

Tanya watched dispassionately while her fate was being decided. She had seen too much, understood too well that appeal to the depraved judge was futile.

"Yeah, I think you would," McGuffin said. "Right after you killed me." He stuck the automatic in his belt and walked across the dining room to the phone beside the glass doors.

"What are you going to do?" Victor called.

"I'm going to call a friend. You might not be all that much impressed by Henry when you meet him, but I think he's one of the keenest criminal minds since Sherlock Holmes," McGuffin said, as he reached for the phone.

Chapter 19

The press had a wonderful time with the Belmont case. As defendants they had a billionaire developer, his playboy brother with a missing pinky and a voluptuous chanteuse whose photogenic cleavage would be marred by neither bars nor starchy prison garb. The story had a mob lawyer, a boobytrapped bomb, an ex-major league ballplayer, a society bookmaker and a beast who extracts debts with a pair of pliers. It was a can't-miss story and everybody on both coasts knew it. Besides being interviewed by scores of newspapers and magazines, McGuffin appeared several times on television, was offered fifty thousand dollars for exclusive story rights, and was besieged with Hollywood film and television offers. Even Andre Hersh phoned, informing McGuffin that he was no longer associated with the Belmont brothers and was free to represent him in negotiations for his story, if McGuffin were willing to let bygones be bygones.

McGuffin informed him that he wasn't but had to ask, "Why are you no longer representing the Belmonts?"

"That's not entirely true," Hersh qualified. "Actually I'm representing Penny Belmont who's about to sue Johnny for divorce. But I have no conflict where you're concerned," he hastened to add. Hersh knew where the money was and went to it like a pointer to pheasants.

McGuffin thanked him but informed him that Franz Tutin

had already arranged for him to sign with the William Morris Agency, which had made Marilyn a bit peevish.

"My agent is a schmuck, he can't even get me a reading, but you who's not even an actor gets signed by the William Morris Agency!" she wailed. "Where's the justice?"

"Take Hillary back to San Francisco and I'll give up show business," McGuffin promised.

But once more Marilyn refused, gathered up her pictures and résumés and set out for the cattle calls, while McGuffin waited for the limousine that would whisk him to the *Donahue Show* along with Henry Dunkel. For although McGuffin was clearly the greatest beneficiary of the Belmont case, he made it a point at every turn to include Henry Dunkel, the unsung property clerk who had the temerity to challenge the FBI Bomb Squad and win. Yet for all that, and despite the brief fame he shared with McGuffin, he was still the underpaid property clerk at the county sheriff's office.

Nor was Tanya treated as fairly as McGuffin thought she deserved. Victor was arraigned by the county prosecutor and released on bail the same day, while Tanya was forced to remain in the county jail until McGuffin went bail for her several days later. He also hired an attorney for her, figuring he owed her at least that much for saving his life. His sworn statement that she had shot Daniels in self-defense, coupled with her willingness to cooperate with the prosecution, would exonerate her of one homicide anyway. For her part in the bombing and Angelo's death, however, she would have to do some time, the amount depending on the quality of her cooperation and the ability of her lawyer to cut a deal.

Johnny Belmont too would have to do some time for his part in Angelo's death, although it was expected that his sentence also would be a relatively lenient one, owing to his reputation as a none-too-bright playboy easily led astray. Some including the prosecuting attorney, after hearing McGuffin's story, even believed that Johnny was almost justified in attempting to kill his brother. For there was no doubt Victor had attempted everything short of homicide to

176

force Johnny out of the family business and, when all else failed, resorted to homicide. The public had watched Victor Belmont acquire a fortune greater than that of some countries, bribing and intimidating city officials, driving tenants from their homes, often borrowing the money from the very banks in which these people had deposited their savings, and they were eager for the head of the king of the developers.

Eager as they were, however, the wheels of justice turned slowly. For several weeks McGuffin was scarcely aware of the passing of time, so preoccupied was he with the offices of celebrity—television appearances, forty-dollar haircuts, meetings with his agent and trips to the coast—but once discarded by the fickle public, the days grew longer and duller. Only Hillary, who confessed to her father that she was thinking of giving up the stage to become a lady detective, remained in thrall to his exploits when the others had deserted him. She accompanied him when he drove upstate to confer with the prosecuting attorney and went along to lunch with Henry Dunkel, a "neato detective," even if he was just a property clerk.

"I think something good will happen for Henry some day, don't you, Dad?" she asked one day, while they waited in Orso's Restaurant for her mother.

"Sure," McGuffin replied unenthusiastically. His agent had just informed him that six bankable stars had read the film script of the Belmont case, and they had all declined the role of Amos McGuffin. It was nothing personal, the agent assured him, but McGuffin was bummed. He was about to educate his daughter to the first of life's harsh realities, that merit is not always rewarded, when her mother fairly ran over the maitre d' and slammed herself in the chair next to Hillary.

"Mommy!" Hillary exclaimed, as McGuffin asked, "What's the matter?"

"That bastard!" she said.

"What bastard?"

"Do you know what he did?"

"Who?"

"He sold it."

"What are you talking about?"

"Franz Tutin—he sold the theater to Laird Strauss."

"No—"

"Yes! The Actors Company is no more. It's closed, finished. The greatest theatrical company in the world has been destroyed by that selfish SOB!"

"What do you mean destroyed, isn't he going to open someplace else?" McGuffin asked.

"Someplace else!" she exclaimed, attracting attention for several tables around. "He's going to Hollywood to make movies!"

"No!" Hillary gasped. "Mr. Tutin hates movies."

"But he loves money as much as anyone else. He says it's time to think of his old age. Can you imagine? Waiter!" she shouted. "And that's not all," she added, turning a defeated face to McGuffin. "Lance is back in town."

"Lance—?"

"The actor I'm subletting the apartment from? The one who was doing *The Desert Song* in Australia?"

"Yeah—?"

"He ran off with an Australian chorus boy and he wants the apartment back by the end of the week. Double martini," she snapped at the waiter.

"He can't do that, you've got a lease," McGuffin said.

She shook her head. "It's not legal to sublet a rent-controlled apartment, all we did was shake on it."

"We'll get a lawyer."

"I don't want a lawyer, I want to go home."

"Home—?" McGuffin repeated. It was what he had been dying to hear for months, yet he was suddenly unnerved at the prospect.

"Back to San Francisco?" Hillary asked.

"I'm sorry, darling, but your father is right, I never should have brought you to New York. It's a place of deceit and disillusionment," she said, then turned to McGuffin. "Forgive me, Amos. I was thinking only of myself and I didn't

178

even get that right. I'm a competent community theater actress and that's all. I've tromped all over this city, auditioned for every director, every theater company, every film, every commercial casting director, and everywhere I get the same message. Go back, it'll destroy you. Well, I'm not going to let it destroy my daughter or you, Amos. I'm ready to go back first thing in the morning. Hell, I'll go back right now, just as soon as I've finished my martini. Where the hell is that martini?" she shouted at the passing waiter.

"Oh, God! To think I used to wonder why we got divorced. I'm amazed you put up with me as long as you did. First the painting, then the poetry, then the singing and finally the acting. Me me me! I was a cultural yuppie and didn't know it. Is it too late to say I'm sorry? Deeply and truly sorry."

"You don't have to apologize, Mom."

"And I don't think you should quit."

"What—?"

"Nobody becomes a star overnight, it takes years."

"Years! You're the guy who told me artists shouldn't be encouraged because it only prolongs the agony of defeat," she reminded him, as the waiter hurried to their table with her double martini.

"Maybe I was wrong. Look at me, struggling at my profession for eighteen years, doing decent work but never getting that one break. Until one day, bang, the Fabergé egg falls in my lap. One minute Sam Spade, the next Nick Charles."

"And I'm Nora," she said, lifting her double martini.

"Persistence breeds luck," McGuffin continued. "Stay with it, Marilyn. Stay with it and it'll happen," he promised.

"You mean you don't want to go back to San Francisco?" she asked, halting her lift.

"That's not what I'm saying. All I'm saying is we should give it some time," he said, not sure what he was saying. "There are a lot of things happening now that weren't happening before."

"Such as—?"

179

"The trial, for one. I have to be here to testify."

"That might take months—you can fly back for that."

"And there's the movie."

"They don't need you for that."

But they do, McGuffin thought, as Marilyn went on listing the reasons they should return posthaste to San Francisco. It suddenly dawned on him that the six leading men the agency had approached were entirely wrong. They were performers who made a career of rough, hardbitten, hard-drinking, down-at-the-heels types of roles—the kinds of parts that forty years ago would have gone to Humphrey Bogart. But that wasn't Amos McGuffin, at least not anymore. Now he had style, he lived in a classy hotel in the most sophisticated city in the world. They shouldn't be looking for Bogart, they should be looking for William Powell. He would phone the Morris Agency first thing in the morning and tell them.

"My good man," he called to the waiter. "Would you bring me a double martini, very dry with two olives?"

"Amos!" Marilyn cried at this interruption of her brief.

"Oh—and another for Nora," he added.